SCI-FI JUNIOR HIGH

CRASH LANDING

JOHN MARTIN   **SCOTT SEEGERT**

Scholastic Children's Books
An imprint of Scholastic Ltd
Euston House, 24 Eversholt Street, London, NW1 1DB, UK
Registered office: Westfield Road, Southam, Warwickshire, CV47 0RA
SCHOLASTIC and associated logos are trademarks and/or
registered trademarks of Scholastic Inc.

First published in the US by Jimmy Patterson Books/Little,
Brown and Company, 2018
First published in the UK by Scholastic Ltd, 2018

ISBN 978 1407 18001 4

A CIP catalogue record for this book
is available from the British Library.

Printed by CPI Group (UK) Ltd, Croydon, CR0 4YY
Papers used by Scholastic Children's Books are made
from wood grown in sustainable forests.

1 3 5 7 9 10 8 6 4 2

www.scholastic.co.uk

To Margie and Mary, who have had the good grace, and questionable judgement, to spend the majority of their lives with a couple of perpetual twelve-year-olds

Day 1

329 QUADRILLION
MILES FROM
EARTH...

 "All right, everybody. Gather round. Remember yesterday, when I told you we'd be climbing something tomorrow? Something no one has ever been able to make it to the top of in all the years I've been teaching gym classes? Well, *today* is tomorrow, and what we'll be climbing is this rope right here."

Yeah, Coach Ed, I remember yesterday, all right. And so does my buddy Rand-El.

That's when he came up with the idea to make this my one big thing, the thing I'll always be remembered for. Kelvin Klosmo—the guy who made it to the top.

"And I hope you all took my advice and did a few extra push-ups before you went to bed last night, because you're going to need every bit of strength you can muster to get up this baby. It's wobbly, it's slippery, and it's over thirty feet high."

You see, we figure that if I become known for something really cool, everybody will forget about how I tried to fake being superbrilliant when I first got to this new school at the far end of the galaxy. And then maybe they'll quit calling me Genius. You know, the sarcastic kind. Like when you call a short kid Paul Bunyan. Or a shy kid Mr. Personality. At least, that's the theory. The teasing is getting pretty unbearable.

"Now let me give you a few pointers. I don't mean to brag, but I *was* the Delpneer District pole climbing champion back in eighty-seven. So I know what I'm talking about."

I asked Rand-El, if no one else ever made it to the top, why did he think I could? I'm no athlete. I mean, if my backpack's full, I have trouble climbing into the shuttle bus in the morning.

He told me not to sweat it, that he had it all taken care of.

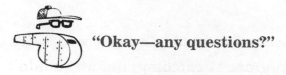 "Okay—any questions?"

 "Yeah, are we allowed to keep our arms attached to our bodies?"

 "Sure . . . if you want to do it the *easy* way. Now, who's going to go first?"

Danny Diptera. He's known for his sticky fingers. And I don't mean I-got-some-jelly-on-my-hands sticky. I'm talking I-dumped-a-gallon-of-glue-on-myself-and-then-fell-into-avat-of-tar sticky. I tried playing catch with him once. He was great at catching, but he couldn't throw the ball back. And no matter how many times he says, "Lay it on me, dude," you do *not* want to high-five Danny Diptera. Trust me on that one. He should be able to scramble up that rope, no problem. No matter how slippery it is.

Danny makes it to the seven-foot mark and slides back down. It takes ten minutes to unstick him from the cushions.

Zot volunteers to go next. She's the best ath-lete I've ever seen. If anybody can do this, she can. Come to think of it, maybe I should have just asked her to wear a Kelvin mask for her climb to the top.

Zot makes it to the ten-foot mark and that's it. What's this rope made out of, anyway? Vaseline?

I nudge Rand-El. "Great idea you've got here. I'll be lucky to get my feet off the ground."

Rand-El hands me something.

 "What are these?"

"Antigravity discs. My mom uses them to rearrange the furniture in our LIV space. Stick them in your boots. When it's your turn on the rope, just kick your feet together and they'll turn on. You'll practi-cally fly to the top of that rope!"

You know what? Rand-El might actually have something here. I shove the discs into my boots and volunteer to go next. After spitting into my hands and rubbing them together for effect, I grab on to the rope and kick my feet together. And suddenly I feel weightless. I start to climb.

Dang! This might actually work!

Now that's more like it! Good-bye Genius.
Hello Climbing Kelv.

Ugh. The Drifting Doofus? Are you kidding me?

 "Thanks a lot, Rand-El."

 "Hey, it's better than Genius."

 "Really, Rand-El? Is it? That's like saying a stubbed big toe is better than *two* stubbed big toes. It might be a little bit better, but it still hurts. A lot."

"Hey, look, everybody! It's the Drifting Doofus *Genius!*"

And *that* hurts like *five* stubbed big toes.

Yikes! I must have been daydreaming again. Nowadays that's the only time I answer anything right.

*"**Who** is you, Mr. Klosmo. **What** is telling the class how many there are. And **when** is right this instant!"*

How many *what* there are? Man, I hate galactic geography. Looks like it's guess time again. Should I go high or low this time? Low, I think.

"Uh ... three?"

"Three? Am I to understand, Mr. Klosmo, that you believe there are only three planets in the entire Milky Way galaxy? Your own solar system has eight all by itself. Nine

if you count Pluto. Would you like to take another stab at it?"

Of course I wouldn't. Problem is, when Professor Plutz asks a question like that, it sounds like you have a choice, but you really don't. At least I know what the question *is* now, even if I don't have a clue about the answer. Who knows . . . maybe I'll get lucky. Let's see—I know the space station has families from over two hundred different planets living aboard it, so there must be at least that many. Add in a few more here and there and I should at least be pretty close.

"Three hundred?"

"Actually, Mr. Klosmo, there are over one hundred *billion* planets in our galaxy."

Oops . . .

That's Dorn. I have no idea why he hates me so much, but at least he hasn't stuffed me into my helmet lately. Not since Grimnee wadded him up in that ball of desks a couple months ago. Grimnee *hates* bullies.

And there's that word again. "Genius." And like I said, they aren't using it the way they did when I first got here, when everybody thought I really *was* one. And why wouldn't they? My parents are the top two scientists on the entire planet Earth. It only makes sense that their son would bump that up a notch and be even smarter, right? It's only natural to assume that he would be what I like to call a Mighty Mega Supergenius. And I sure wasn't going to be the one to let on any differently, especially since it made me a pretty big deal around school. I mean, people *expected* it.

But a guy can only pretend to be smart for so long, and now the cat's out of the bag and my reputation's taken a real nosedive. I mean, talk about your crash landing. Everybody knows I'm pretty average and, after that last answer, maybe not even that. That's why I'm getting the other "genius" treatment. I'm not giving up hope, though. I'm sure my brainpower is going to kick in at some point. Well . . . pretty sure. Actually, I guess desperate wishing is more where I am at this point.

For now, though, maybe I can still save face. . . .

"Uh, I actually thought you meant *inhabited* **planets, Professor."**

 "If I had meant inhabited planets, Mr. Klosmo, I would have let you know as much by including the term 'inhabited' in the question."

"Well, then I'd like to change my answer to one hundred billion."

"And I'd like to retire to the silicon beaches of Shnurlor, Mr. Klosmo. But that isn't going to happen, either. I suggest you spend less time daydreaming and more time studying if you wish to pass this class. It's not like you're a genius, you know."

YEAH. I KNOW.

ell, that was fun. Nothing like a morning of embarrassing yourself in front of a couple classes to get the old digestive juices flowing. And it looks like I'm going to need every drop to process today's lunch "special."

You know, maybe I'm being too hard on myself. At least with Plutz's class. Since it's the last one before lunch, a lot of the kids were probably zoning out there at the end like they usually do. There's a good chance nobody but Dorn was even paying attention to what was going on.

"How would you know, Zot? You're not even in the class. And neither are you, Rand-El."

"I heard about it from Gil."

"I heard about it from Zot."

"And I heard about it from the lunch ladies."

"The lunch ladies? Wait. Spotch, you're actually *in* the class."

"I know, but I was zoning out there at the end like I usually do. It *is* the last class before lunch."

So, now even the lunch ladies know about my intellectual failures. And they aren't shy about passing it on. I guess when you're famous for being a genius, you're just as famous for being the guy who's not. At least there's less pressure now. It takes a lot of effort to fake being a genius. Not being one is pretty easy. A little too easy in my case.

 "You know, guys, it's really getting old being the *non*genius genius."

"Well, Kelvin, we all said your secret was safe with us. You're the one who decided to tell the entire school about it. People don't like to feel duped."

 "I know. But I couldn't keep faking it forever. The pressure was driving me nuts. And I swear I started losing some hair. But I can't spend the rest of my time here being the moron genius, either."

"That's why you need to do that *one big thing,* like we talked about

the other day. Something amazing that you'll be remembered for
forever."

"Yeah. Like when Rand-El accidentally fell down that garbage chute."

MIPPITT, SHUT
DOWN ALL OF THE
GARBAGE COMPACTORS
ON PRINCIPAL ORT'S
DETENTION LEVEL!

"Hey, Gil! I was tripped! Besides,
there's no way anybody remembers that!"

"Speaking of that one big thing, how did it go in Coach Ed's class? Rand-El said he had a foolproof plan."

"Turns out no plan involving Rand-El is ever *fool*proof."

"Isn't that the truth. Everybody say hello to the Drifting Doofus."

"Drifting Doofus. Funny!"

"Vvvvvvt. Beeeeep."

Today was a disaster, no doubt. But I really do think the guys are onto something. I just need to become famous for doing one superamazing, totally awesome thing! Something nobody's ever seen or done before. Just hopefully not odour related, like Rand-El. All that "genius" junk would be a thing of the past. Well, at least until the real thing actually kicks in. Which it will. Someday. Right?

Finally! School never seems to fly by, but on days where you humiliate yourself it can last forever. I can't wait to get back home and play with Lightyear for a while. But first Dad wants me to meet him down in his laboratory to help him carry some boxes back to our LIV space, so I head for the elevator.

He hasn't allowed me back into the lab since that whole disaster with the robot. Which is totally unfair. Sure, we almost died from the cold, lack of oxygen, and giant robot hand lasers. But we also saved the *whole, entire universe!* Which would be really impressive . . . if anybody actually believed we did it.

I reach the elevator and push the down button. It's always crowded in this part of the space station, so sometimes you have to wait for three or four full cars to pass you by before getting on. I sure hope that's not the case this time. You know that whole chilling-out-with-Lightyear thing I mentioned? Forget it—suddenly that "special" I had for lunch has me thinking more about the bathroom right now. The elevator stops and the doors open. Turns out there's good news and bad news. The good news is there's only one person riding it. The bad news is . . .

I can think of fifty thousand things I'd rather do than get on that elevator. But that "special" in my gut makes the decision for me. "Uh . . . yeah," I say, quickly stepping over a couple tentacles and into a sort-of-dry spot in the back corner.

"Where to?" my copassenger asks.

"Level L three," I answer.

"L three? That's where all the laboratories are. Are you sure you're supposed to be down there?"

"My dad is head of the robotics department. I'm meeting him after school." Just push the button, already, will ya? What's the deal with this guy?

"Robotics?" he says. "I knew you looked familiar. You're Professor Klosmo's son, aren't you?"

"Yeah," I tell him. "I'm Kelvin." My stomach is starting to make some very alarming sounds. PUSH THE BUTTON!

"Ah, yes. Kelvin Klosmo—boy genius. Or should I say *former* boy genius?"

Oh, c'mon! Even *this* guy knows? I'm about to jump back off the elevator when a dripping tentacle reaches over to the control panel and presses L3. No sooner do the doors close than . . .

Holy egg rot, that had to be my worst one ever! This is so embarrassing. And I'm still stuck in here for six more levels. Hey, wait a minute! What if *this* ends up being the one big thing that makes me famous—the thing that everybody remembers forever? The Flatulent Fool. The Gassy Goof. *No, no, no, no, no!* This would be Rand-El times a *thousand!* I've got to nip this in the bud. I know—I could tell him I'm sick, which is sort of true anyway, and beg him not to tell anybody. Yeah, that might work. No grown-up would make fun of a sick kid, would they? I'm just about to apologize when . . .

The doors slide open and I claw my way out into the sweet, lifesaving recycled air of the corridor. I really dodged a bullet there, but only for a minute if I don't find a bathroom. *Fast.*

Meanwhile, a few million miles away . . .

Well, it's about time I freed myself from that absurd asteroid! Two months stuck playing tea party with that gargantuan goofball was sixty days too long. Fortunately, I was able to escape by using parts from my disabled giant robot to create this magnificent handship, which I shall call my . . . um . . .

Handship

Nah. That's clearly no good. It sounds like something my archnemesis Klosmo would have come up with. Perhaps if I add a bit of alliteration, it will seem more menacing. Yes! Now we're getting somewhere. I shall instead call it my . . .

Harrowing Handship

Better, but still nothing to write home about. There must be something . . . I've got it! I will add an evil laugh and a few exclamation points and call it my . . .

Harrowing Handship!!! BWAHAHAHA!!!

Now THAT'S more like it! Quite fearsome sounding indeed. You tell someone you'll be stopping by in your Harrowing Handship!!! BWAHAHAHA!!! and that person just might require a change of underwear.

And now on to my first destination—the

planetoid Zurton. There I shall _finally_ retrieve the all-powerful Zorb and use it to rule the universe! Only two short months ago I had that gleaming globe mere _inches_ from my grasp, only to be foiled by Klosmo's kid and his misfit friends.

And there's the planetoid now!

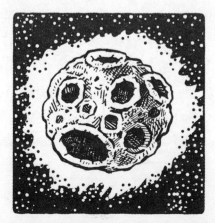

The Zorb should be just over that ridge. I can practically feel its power running through my veins . . . er . . . cotton stuffing already. Let's see . . . what should I conquer first? The space station? Earth, perhaps? Maybe an entire solar system! There are so many evil choices!

What is this?! _It's gone!_ zarfloots, ZAR-FLOOTS, _ZARFLOOTS!!_ This can only be the work of klosmo! I remember seeing that crane in his laboratory. That sorry excuse for a scientist must have found a way to retrieve the zorb without turning himself into mush. or maybe he _did_ turn into mush during the process of retrieving it. Ha, I should be so lucky. He must have it back with him on that despicable space station. Drat! I was hoping never to set foot upon that miserable mass of metal again.

Thať was a close one! I grab my backpack and head down the corridor to my parents' laboratory. Dad's waiting for me at the entrance.

The needle on Dad's hilariosity meter is still stuck down there around zero. He thinks he's hysterical, though. And, for some strange reason, so do the other kids at Sci-Fi Junior High. He's become sort of a legend out here in space.

 "It, uh, took me a while to catch an elevator. They were really crowded."

"Don't I know it. I'll tell you, though—you get the chance to

**meet some really interesting folks
riding those things."**

Yeah. *Interesting*. Tell that to my nose hairs.

 "So, what's going on? I thought I
wasn't allowed down here anymore."

 "Oh, you're not. Not after that stunt
you pulled with my robot. But I'm
making an exception today. I can't
carry all these boxes myself."

 "But, Dad, we also saved the universe from whoever was piloting
your robot!"

 "Well . . . maybe. But you *were* running pretty low on oxygen when
we found you. Who knows what
tricks your mind may have been
playing on you."

"Tricks? That robot almost got the Zorb, Dad. Ask Spotch. Or Zot. Or anybody else who was there."

 "Well, you were *all* low on oxygen."

"What, *that* container? Uh . . . nothing."

 "Then why is it being guarded by robots?"

"Well . . . er . . . you see, it's just that . . . um . . . aw, heck with it. It's the Zorb, Kelvin."

 "WHAT?! It's here? On the space station? But I thought it turned any living thing that got near it to goo! YIKES— like that poor guy over there!"

"Oh. That's Stevens. He always looks like that."

IT'S TRUE.

"That vault you're looking at is made of impenetranium, which blocks the Zorb's energy. And it's three feet thick, so nobody is breaking into it. Not even your mother if you tell her it's filled with chocolate-covered cherries. HAR!"

"And I'm the only one who can get anywhere near it. The robots will scan any intruder that approaches the vault, and unless they exactly match my physical appearance, well . . . just watch this."

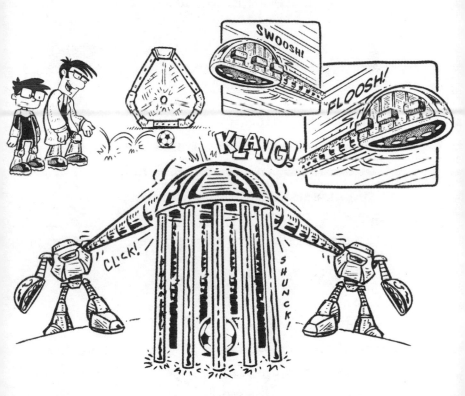

"Anyway, that should calm any fears you might have about someone stealing the Zorb and using it for no good."

"Not just for no good, Dad. For *conquering the universe!* That's what Zot heard the guy in the robot's control dome say. That's why you should just destroy it. It's too dangerous."

"But that's exactly why we *can't* destroy it, Kelvin. We need to examine it and study it and learn how to harness its power for the good of everyone in the galaxy. It's completely safe, Kelvin. There's absolutely nothing to worry about."

Nothing to worry about? Hasn't he seen those movies where some scientist is working on a formula or something that he swears is safe, and then it turns a ladybug into a giant monster that eats Delaware? Or a scientist is working on a cure for hiccups that he swears is safe, and then he spills it down the drain and into the water supply and everybody turns into two-headed zombies? Why don't grown-ups get this stuff?

I spend the whole walk back to the LIV space trying to convince Dad what a horrible idea it is to keep that Zorb. I even tell him about those movies I saw.

"Well, son," he says, "I used to watch *The Three Stooges* when I was a kid. You don't see me worrying about having a pie thrown in my face or getting poked in the eye with a rake handle, now do you? HAR!"

Glad to see he's taking this so seriously.

"Look, Kelvin. I understand your concern, but

everything is going to be fine. You'll just have to trust me on this one."

Yup. That's just what those movie scientists would say.

We reach the door to our unit. I wonder if Mom's home yet. She left the lab early to pick Bula up from preschool. Maybe *she'll* have enough sense to see my side of things. Mom, that is. Bula doesn't have enough sense to put her underwear on frontward. How she ended up in this family, I'll never know.

"Uh-oh. What did you get into this time, Lightyear?"

Dad brought Lightyear home from one of the labs a couple months ago. He had lapped up a puddle of what they call matter replication liquid, so now he barfs up exact duplicates of whatever he happens to be looking at when he's eating. Like his ball. And he'll eat anything, including rocks. Sure, it's gross. But it's awesome, too!

"I'll clean this up," I say to Dad.

"Okeydokes," Dad says. "I'll order a new seat cushion and start dinner."

When Dad says "*start* dinner," he means pick out the picture of whatever food we want for tonight.

"*Make* dinner" means pushing the Select button on the food synthesizer. "*Skip* dinner" is what I usually feel like doing, since everything tastes exactly the same—like pencil erasers. Even the hot-fudge-covered chocolate chip brownies.

I pick up the cushion balls and take them to my room. I've got a whole dresser drawer filled with these things made out of everything from tooth-brushes to dirty socks. Hey, you never know when you might need a ball made out of glass (Mom's favourite vase) or wood (Mom and Dad's wedding picture frame) or synthesized grilled cheese (Bula's lunch).

I can't really get mad at Lightyear, though. I mean, he's already used his special talent to save my life once, so he gets some leeway. And he's also responsible for my awesome trophy collection.

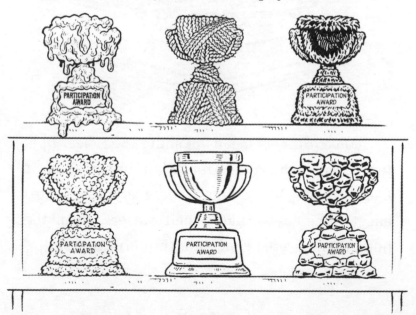

I hear the whoosh of the front door sliding open.

WE'RE HOME!

It's Mom and Bula, home from preschool. Before she even gets the chance to put her bag down, I hit Mom up with my whole Zorb-must-be-destroyed pitch. I give her everything I've got, including some very convincing hand gestures and facial expressions. I even throw in the movie references. She's holding her chin in her hand, so I know I'm getting through to her! Now she's nodding her head! Yes! With her on my side, I know we can change Dad's mind on this!

 **"I understand your concern, Kelvin, but I'm afraid I'm with your father on this. Everything will be fine. There's absolutely nothing to worry about. You'll just have to trust us on this one."**

Gee, where have I heard *that* before? I guess this is the downside to having *both* your parents be scientists. Now what am I supposed to do? And why is Bula grinning at me like that?

 **"Anyway, we have some news. You know how Bula was having trouble focusing in class?"**

Because she's got a hamster wheel instead of a brain? Yeah.

 "Well, they **did** a special evaluation to figure out what was going on. You know what they found?"

I'm sticking with the hamster wheel thing.

 "Our little Bula here . . . is a *genius!*"

Phllupp!

FWOOSH!

You know, if Klosmo ever decided to become an _evil_ genius, he'd probably make a pretty good one. Well, aside from the terrible jokes. He has the Zorb, after all. But the guy is such a Goody Two-shoes. I'm sure he's planning to "examine" it and "study" it and "learn how to harness its power for the good of everyone in the universe." Blech. What a putz.

But all the better for me! While Klosmo wastes his time _not_ using the Zorb to conquer the universe, I, Erik Failenheimer, shall swoop in and take it for myself. But how? He'll have it under constant guard. And he certainly isn't going to just hand it over to an evil little plushy bunny, no matter how cute I am. And even if I _am_ in my Harrowing Handship!!! BWAHAHAHA!!! (I must admit—that does sound impressive!)

No, I must find a way to make him give it to me somehow. Think, Erik. You're a brilliant diabolical genius. This should be as simple as tying your shoes.

Okay . . . bad example. Zarfloots! Coming up with a brilliant evil plan is more difficult than it would seem sometimes. This reminds me of when I was a child and my older brother, Karl, had that container of growth serum that I wanted so badly for myself. He finally gave it to me, but only after I agreed to trade my bike for it.

Not such a bargain, really, since it ended up being a baby food jar filled with cranberry juice. If I ever see Karl again, I'll . . . wait a minute! _That's_ _it!_ I simply need to trade Klosmo something more valuable to him than the Zorb! But what would that be?

Hmm. Possible, but by no means a sure thing. On the other hand . . .

YES! Now we're talking! If I capture his very own son, Melvin or Delvin or whatever the little goober's name is, Klosmo will have no choice but to fork over the Zorb in exchange for him! And I'm still a few hours away from the space station, so I have plenty of time to come up with the details of a kidnapping plan.

All right. I know I shouldn't say this. I realize it hasn't worked out too well for me in the past. But it's a confidence thing. And it really gets my evil juices flowing! Not to mention, every diabolical genius throughout the annals of history has proclaimed these words on his or her way to ultimate evil glory. So why not Erik Failenheimer? I'm brilliant! I'm evil! And (fingers crossed!) . . . <u>NOTHING CAN STOP ME NOW!!</u>

Wait! What's this?! My Harrowing Handship!!! BWAHAHAHA!!!'s instruments have all gone dead!

DAY 2

"**N**ah," I say. "Something came up yesterday that kind of made me forget about the unforgettable thing for a while."

"What?" Spotch says. "I thought that was the top priority. Job number one. What could be more important than that?"

I lay it on him. "My dad has the Zorb in his lab."

"What? THE Zorb? That's impossible. We'd all be goo by now."

Although he doesn't sound like it, Spotch must really be upset with this news. I actually saw one of his eyebrows move.

"He's got it in some kind of special container so he can study it. He says not to worry, that it's completely safe."

Spotch isn't any more convinced than I was. "That's what the scientists always say right before something unexpected happens and everyone grows an extra head and turns into a zombie."

Wow. Movies must be the same everywhere.

"Kelvin, we have to do something! You have to convince your dad to destroy that Zorb! Doesn't he realize how close we came to disaster once already?"

This time an eyelid rises a tiny bit. I think Spotch is starting to lose it.

"I tried," I tell him. "But he isn't going to listen to me. He says it's too important."

Spotch pauses for a second. Then he looks straight at me. "Well," he says, "then we'll just have to figure out some way to get rid of it ourselves."

Us?! Destroy the Zorb?! I'd be grounded forever! But if we don't, somebody like that wacko in the giant robot could get ahold of it, and I'd be stuck mining grismak crystals or floobin ore twenty hours a day for the rest of my life.

PICK UP THE PACE THERE, GENIUS.

Spotch is right.

"You're right," I tell him. "But how would we do that?"

"I don't know," he says. "But we both know somebody who might."

Brian Stem! Smartest kid in the school . . . unless he gets nervous and his brain shrivels up like a raisin.

What's this? A dance? All thoughts of the Zorb disappear as I picture myself gliding around the dance floor with Luna. But that thought starts to fade when I remember I can't dance. Then it totally disappears when I realize there's no way she'd agree to dance with the school's resident nongenius genius anyway.

Okay, so now it looks like I have *three* things on my to-do list:

1. Do something really memorable so I'm popular again and Luna will be impressed enough to dance with me.
2. Learn some actual moves so she doesn't run away after four seconds.
3. Destroy the Zorb.

And it's pretty obvious which one is most important right now.

So the dance is this Thoosday. That's only five days away. I don't think I mentioned it before, but out here a week is eleven days long. Eight school days and a three-day weekend. And days last twenty-two hours. Minutes and seconds are all goofed up, too. Just thinking about it gives me a headache.

I fill up my lunch tray and head over to our table. It looks like everybody else is already there.

Whoa. Did that really just happen? Luna Reeklipps asked *me* if *I* was going to the dance? I'm pretty sure the artificial gravity is still on, but I feel like I'm floating the rest of the way to the table.

"Hey, Kelvin! Snap out of it! Spotch just told us about the Zorb! We've got to get rid of that thing, like, yesterday. Being turned into goo is bad enough, but goo floating around in a ball of water? That's just nasty."

"Not to mention the whole destruction-of-the-universe thing if it falls into the wrong hands. What's your dad thinking? He might be brilliant, but he's not very smart."

The Luna-induced fog in my head clears away with the sound of panic at the table. The Zorb is more important than her interest in me. Slightly. I guess.

"Sure wish you really were the supergenius we all thought you were right about now, Kelvin."

Don't I know it. But at least I do have brains enough to know who *can* help us.

"Hey, I agree with you guys. Spotch and I already talked about it. We figured Brian was the only one smart enough to come up with any ideas."

"Actually, I may have something. Give me a couple days to think about it."

"A couple days? We could be oozing down a drain by then."

Nice going, Gil. That's all we need right now is a nervous Brian Stem. His brain will shrink down to the size of a grape and his solution will be to throw pickles at the Zorb.

"Don't worry about it, Brian. Take your time and we'll see what you come up with in a couple days. Right now we all have classes to get to."

"Yup. And you have something to become known for, Kelv."

Oh yeah. In all the Luna and Zorb excitement, I almost forgot.

It's dinnertime, and I'm rolling my synthesized peas around on my plate with my knife. It's a technique I've been working on for a couple weeks now. When no one is looking, I bat a pea or two onto the floor for Lightyear to gobble up. Then it's a carrot. So far, so good. I'm about to test my luck with the synthesized meat loaf when I notice Mom looking at me.

"So, Kelvin, it looks like you and Bula will be schoolmates starting next week."

"Schoolmates? But Bula's preschool is over here on the space station."

"She won't be in preschool next week. They're moving her up to the second grade. Isn't it exciting?"

"Wait . . . what?" I nearly fall off my chair. "Second grade? But she's only four. On our trip out here she didn't even know what eighteen divided by three was."

"Well," Mom says, "the people who tested her said her geniusness must have . . . now, what was the term they used . . . oh, yes—*kicked in* at some point in the past week or so."

Kicked in? I was right! That *is* how it happens!

"They also said it's possible she could advance three or four grades a year for the next few years."

Okay. Now I actually do fall off my chair. And

I land right on the carrot that Lightyear was slow to get around to.

"But that means we could be in the same class by tenth grade!"

NINTH, ACTUALLY.

DON'T WORRY, THOUGH. IT WOULD ONLY BE FOR A LITTLE WHILE AND THEN I'D MOVE ON TO TENTH GRADE.

This. Cannot. Be. Happening. I get back on my feet and brush the fake carrot off my pants.

"This isn't fair! *I'm* supposed to be the Mighty Mega Supergenius, and Bula is supposed to have a hamster wheel for a brain. Everybody's already calling me Genius because I'm not one. Now my little sister is going to pass me up in school? When is it my turn? When is *my* increased brainpower going to kick in?"

Bula still has that annoying grin on her face. "Maybe it already did. Maybe that's how you got up to average."

I throw a synthesized pea at Bula. I miss, of course, so I guess being known as the guy with the great pea-throwing arm is out.

Mom gives me that you-did-not-really-just-throw-a-pea look. "Actually, Kelvin, I asked about that very thing. They said it could happen any time now. Maybe. They said that yours might kick in at some point soon. Possibly."

"Maybe? Might? Possibly? Where's the 'will'? The 'definitely'? The 'certainly, positively, without a doubt'?"

"Well, Kelvin," Dad chimes in, "you just never know with these things. Not everyone is a genius, you know."

No, but everybody in *my* family is. Except me.

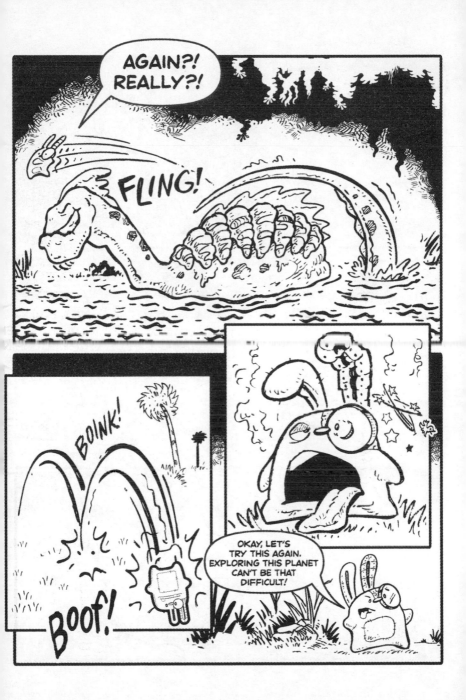

DAY 3

 "My stomach won't stop growling. I'm so hungry I could eat a horse."

"Horse? What's that?"

 "Oh, it's an animal we have back on Earth."

"And you eat it when you're real hungry?"

 "What? Heck no. We ride them, mostly."

"But you said—"

 "We don't actually *eat* horses. It's just a figure of speech. You know, because they're so big."

"So you don't eat big animals on Earth?"

 "Sure we do. Like cows, for instance."

"Then why don't you say you're so hungry you could eat a cow?"

 "I don't know. That's just how the saying goes. We do have a cow saying, too, though—'Don't have a cow.'"

"*Don't* have a cow'? So you say that to people who *aren't* hungry?"

 "Nope. We say that to people who are really upset about something."

"Your planet is weird."

"I guess I could give you my dessert, too. I'm pretty full."

 "I didn't see any dessert. What is it?"

"I'm not sure, but the sign said 'Lava Cake.'"

 "Lava cake? Really? That's my favourite back on Earth! My mom always makes it on my birthday. It's like a mini chocolate cake filled with gooey chocolate syrup. I can't believe they have it out here. I could eat a whole tray of that stuff!"

"A whole tray? Now *that* would be something to see."

"Sure would!"

"Hey, you know what? You guys are right. That really *would* be something to see. Right, Kelvin?"

 "Well, I guess so. But—"

"*Everybody* would be talking about it."

I don't know if I like where this is going.

"Gil is right, Kelv. Maybe *this* can be your big thing."

 "Oh, really, Rand-El. As big as your rope climbing idea? That one sure worked out great."

ISN'T THAT THE DRIFTING DOOFUS? WHAT A *GENIUS*.

"Hey, you're the one who wanted to be known for something. And you said there's not a lot you're good at, right? You're going to have to be creative."

Crud. They're right. I don't have a lot of options. And I really do love lava cake. I ate three of them last year on my birthday. Maybe I *can* do this. Drifting Doofus Genius. Ugh. I've got to give it a try.

"All right, let's do it."

"Oh, this is going to be fantastic! Grimnee and I will get the cakes. She's tight with Mrs. Forzork, the lunch lady."

"And I'll roll around and spread the word!"

Okay. You can do this, Kelvin. Sure, the whole

gym class rope thing was a disaster, but this time it's all on me. None of Rand-El's brain-dead tricks to deal with. All I have to do is chow down on my favourite dessert of all time. This should be a cinch!

Now, where are those two with my tray of cakes?

I have to admit, they do look delicious. And the cafeteria doesn't serve synthesized stuff like back at our LIV space. Gil has delivered a pretty big crowd. Everybody in the lunchroom must be gathered around our table, looking at me.

What the heck. I play it up a bit. I get out of my chair, do a few stretches and toe touches, and sit back down. I give the crowd a nice "Mmmm" and rub my palms together. I grab the first cake, check it out from a few different angles, and take a big bite.

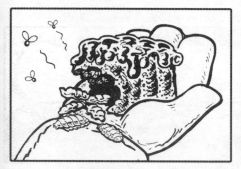 

 "This isn't lava cake!"

"Well, that's what the sign said."

I turn and look over my shoulder toward Mrs. Forzork, who has dessert duty today.

Larva cake?! Seriously?! Even out here on the other end of the galaxy, who is going to eat *larva* cake?!

"Hey, look! It's the Drifting Doo-fus Larva Boy Genius!"

DAY 4

Well, that was a rough night. Biting into a clump of larvae is bad, but having your brain torture you by *thinking* about it for the rest of the day is worse. I tried going to bed early, but every time I fell asleep, I dreamed that a giant larva was eating a cupcake full of tiny Kelvins and woke up screaming. The fresh air of this field trip is just what I need right now.

Mr. Jeddee, our science teacher, is taking us to a nearby planet with an atmosphere close to what we have on the space station, so we won't have to wear our helmets while we're there. He said one of the scientists discovered it by accident when her ship lost control and she had to make an emergency landing on it. I guess the planet emits some kind of pulse or something that messes with a ship's controls when you get too close to it. Supposedly, they figured out how to protect against it now. I hope so. Fresh air is overrated when your face is planted into the side of a cliff.

Assuming we don't crash, we're going to study

the planet's indigenous life-forms. That's a fancy word that means life-forms that are originally from that planet and not brought there from someplace else. And Mr. Jeddee let Lightyear come along, too, which is great because he hasn't had a chance to run around loose in forever.

We've got all the choice seats in the back of the bus, too. Dorn tried to save the last couple rows for himself . . . but Grimnee discussed the situation with him and convinced him to relocate.

It's going to be a while before we land, and Brian's pretty large brained right now, so I figure it's a good time to see how he's coming along with his Zorb destruction plans.

"Actually, they're right here in my pocket."

PLAN TO DESTROY ZORB BEFORE IT FALLS INTO THE WRONG HANDS

step 1. Have Lightyear regurgitate a copy of Professor Klosmo made of polyurethane.

step 2. Sneak into lab when empty and make way over to Zorb containment vault using Professor Klosmo copy as a shield to fool robotic guards. Tell an extremely funny joke followed with a "HAR!" to ensure success.

step 3. Use Zorb energy-neutralization beam to render Zorb powerless.

"Wow. That's amazing."

"I thought you'd be impressed!"

 "No, I mean that you guys *still* actually think my dad's funny."

"Are you kidding? He's hilarious!"

"Yeah, Kelvin. Your dad may be a brilliant scientist, but he'd be an even better stand-up comic."

"I don't know how you live with it. I laugh so hard my stomach hurts just *thinking* about some of those jokes!"

Oh, they make my stomach hurt, too. But in a more nausea-related way. It's like the entire galaxy outside of Earth has a terrible sense of humour. But there may not even *be* a galaxy for long if we don't destroy that Zorb. So back to Brian's plan.

 "I didn't even know there *was* a Zorb energy-neutralization beam."

"Well, technically there isn't. But I have a plan to create one!"

PLAN TO CREATE ZORB ENERGY-NEUTRALIZATION BEAM

Step 1. Have Mippitt collect all known energy-neutralization data.

Step 2. Have Mippitt tap into the Science Hub's computer system and collect all known data on the Zorb.

Step 3. Gain access to beam manufacturing lab and its massive inventory of beam components and technology.

Step 4. Eat pudding.

Step 5. I like pudding.

"Wait! Everything sounded great up until step four. What happened?"

"Well, once I got past step three, I kept thinking about all the terrible things that might happen if this plan doesn't work. And I guess it stressed me out, because my brain shrank to the size of a froop nut. Sorry, guys. Maybe someone else could come up with the rest of the plan."

"Someone else? Come up with the part where we actually design the beam? Like who? I'm having trouble just passing my classes right now. Maybe Grimnee can sing to you again. That kept you calm back a couple months ago when we were trapped in the robot's foot."

"Can't. Sorry."

"Grimnee's got a sore throat. Four of them, actually. She's got a doctor's appointment in the morning."

"Well, I guess we'll just have to figure something else out, then."

Yeah? Like what, Genius?
Oh, great. Now I'm even doing it to myself.

"Look, everybody spend some time tonight brainstorming about how we can destroy that Zorb. We'll go over the ideas at lunch tomorrow. Maybe between all of us we can patch together something that will work."

Right. And maybe my butt will sprout wings and learn to play the ukulele.

"There it is!" I say to Rand-El. "We should be down in a few minutes. I don't know about you, but I can't wait to actually feel dirt and grass under my feet again."

Rand-El looks unimpressed. "What's grass? And how do you know if there even *is* any dirt? What if the whole surface is all soft and mushy?

And wet. I'm wearing my brand-new boots. If I ruin my brand-new boots, my mom is *not* going to be happy."

Good old Rand-El. Always anticipating the best.

"C'mon, Rand-El. Why would Mr. Jeddee bring us to a planet that would ruin all of our footwear?"

"I don't know. Maybe he owns the boot store back on the space station."

I glance over at Rand-El. "Hey, maybe he's going to offer us a boot discount."

We all quiet down, and Mr. Jeddee continues.

"Before we land, we need to go over a few things. I'll be doing a little demonstration later, but before that you're free to go ahead and explore on your own for a while. Two rules. First, stay in groups of at least two. That way, if one of you gets eaten by a Klandarian cronckadile, there will be someone left to tell me about it."

The bus erupts with laughter. For that terrible joke. It's almost as if—

"Just kidding. Professor Klosmo told me to say that. Is he hilarious, or what?"

I knew it!

"Seriously, though, stick together in groups. And rule number two—absolutely, positively DO NOT take anything from the planet. As good galactic citizens, we must leave everything exactly as we found it."

The bus lurches as the retro thrusters begin to

fire. We touch down on what feels, at least, like solid ground.

"A couple more things before we let you out," Mr. Jeddee continues. "This is a relatively small planet, so the gravity is less than what you're used to on the space station and in the school. It may take a little while to adjust to it. And stay away from any bodies of water you run into. Our probes weren't able to analyse them accurately, so we don't know what might be in there."

The driver opens the door. "Be sure that someone from each group takes a com device from the bin on your way out," Mr. Jeddee reminds us. "We'll all meet back here in an hour for the demonstration."

"I don't know, Rand-El. Seems pretty solid to me."

 "We'll see. I already have a little dirt on my left boot."

Wow. There really is less gravity here. This should be fun.

Especially for Lightyear. Wait a minute—where *is* Lightyear?

I t took us a while to track him down, but we finally caught up to Lightyear in a nearby field.

"Well, he's certainly having a marvellous time. Lightyear's instinctual behaviour appears unencumbered down here on the planet's surface."

It's Brian. Big-brained Brian. I guess our field trip is more relaxing for him than thinking about designing a Zorb energy-neutralization beam.

"Uh . . . sure. I mean, I *guess* so." I might know for sure if I had any idea what he was talking about.

We picked our exploring groups back on the bus. I've got Brian and Gil with me. Lightyear, too, who happens to be heading this way with a stick in his mouth. It looks like he wants to play fetch. He drops the stick at my feet, so I bend over to pick it up. And it crawls away and hides behind a log. And then the log gets up, on about twenty legs, and runs behind a big boulder. Well, I have to admit, that's the strangest thing I've seen in a while. And that's coming from somebody who's standing next to a kid whose brain I can watch shrink and grow inside a Plexiglas dome.

"Well, that was . . . different," says Mr. Plexi-Dome himself. The log thingy must have freaked him out a little bit, because his brain's down to half size again. "Maybe we should go."

"All right. Just let me grab Lightyear." Too late. He darts behind the boulder, probably looking for his stick buddy.

"C'mon, Lightyear," I call. "We should start heading back to the landing area."

I'm about to attempt a whistle when Lightyear comes bounding out from behind the boulder. He has something in his mouth, but it's not the stick.

"Hey! What's that?"

 "Heck if I know. Looks like a rock or something."

A really cool *glowing* rock, that is. I pick it up. It's hard and incredibly smooth. Kind of warm, too. And lighter than any rock this size I've ever held before. Rounder, too.

Mom would love this thing. Her birthday's coming up, and it's not like there are a ton of gift options on the space station. At least not in my price range.

Or, better yet, I could give it to Luna! She'd *have* to appreciate something this nice. And maybe the guy who gave it to her, too! I can always get Mom a new kitchen sponge or something. I stuff my glowing ticket to Luna Town into my travel pack.

"You better put that back, Kelvin. Remember what Mr. Jeddee said about not taking anything?"

"Yeah? Well, he also said to stay away from water, and look at Gil over there."

NOW *THIS* IS THE LIFE!

 "What is it with you guys? Didn't you listen to anything Mr. Jeddee said?"

"Aw, relax, Brian. I *live* in the water, remember? If anything weird was going on, don't you think I'd be the first to know?"

122

We don't look back until we're within sight of the bus. And when we do, the "pond" is back to looking like a pond again. And Brian's brain is back to looking like a golf ball.

I pull the glowing maybe-rock back out of my pack and stare at it. Gil's little mishap has me rethinking the intelligence of taking it back home with me. On the one hand, I know nothing about it. Something unexpected and horrible could happen, putting everyone in danger. On the other hand, Luna will probably think it's cool.

I put it back in my pack.

"What is the meaning of this! Put me down this instant!"

"Xf ibwf uif hsfbu pof! Boe if mpplt efmjdjpvt!" (WE HAVE THE GREAT ONE! AND HE LOOKS DELICIOUS!)

Zarfloots! I don't have time to be hauled all over this ridiculous planet by a bunch of oddly shaped nitwits! I have places to go and people to kidnap! Well, one person, anyway. Hey! What was that?! Did one of them just . . . lick me? One of them just licked me!

That darn well better be a sign of respect on this planet, or heads will roll! Wait . . . do they even _have_ heads?

"If't b mpu tnbmmfs uibo J uipvhi if xpvme cf." (HE'S A LOT SMALLER THAN I THOUGHT HE WOULD BE.)

"Zft. Xf ibe cfuufs cf bu uif gspou pg uif mjof jg xf xbou up hfu tpnf." (YES. WE HAD BETTER BE AT THE FRONT OF THE LINE IF WE WANT TO GET SOME.)

"What are you saying? I can't understand you. I think I may have made out the word 'brilliant.' If you happen to be discussing how brilliant I am, I totally agree. And feel free to continue!"

Bah! It's no use. I may as well be talking to an eggplant. If they don't put me down

soon, I know which planet I'm going to conquer first once I get my hands on that Zorb!
what is the point of all this? where are they
taking me?

HELLO.

Our hour of exploration time is up and the rest of the gang meets us back at the clearing.

"Uh . . . what's going on, guys?"

"Not bad, eh? Turns out Grimnee's even stronger on this planet
than she is back at the school."

 "We're all stronger. Because of the
weaker gravity, remember?"

"Whatever. All I know is she's
keeping my boots from getting
dirty. My mom wouldn't be too
happy if my boots got dirty."

Again with the dirt and the boots. Rand-El's
home planet must be completely covered with
carpeting.

Mr. Jeddee calls everybody over. He pops open
a metal case and removes a strange piece of equip-
ment. It must be demonstration time.

 "What I have here is a portable magnetic field generator. As we covered in class last week, a variety of creatures use magnetic fields in order to navigate, including many birds and various types of worms. I'll turn the setting to high and see if we're able to attract a few of them."

GONG!

"Well, that setting may have been *too* high. Let's turn it down just a bit and give it another try."

STILL A TAD TOO HIGH, I WOULD SAY.

"Actually, class, this is an excellent example of trial-and-error experimentation. Now I've moved the dial down to the top end of the worm range. Hopefully, we can coax a few of the little wigglers to make an appearance."

AND THERE'S A LITTLE MORE OF THE ERROR PART.

-WORMS-

"I apologize, class. I probably should have tried this out beforehand. You know what? Just to be on the safe side, let's turn the dial all the way down to the one worm setting and give it one final shot.

ell, that was fun. And exhausting. But it was great being outside again. I almost forgot what it feels like to be in a real atmosphere. The space station's oxygen circulation system is pretty impressive and all, but nothing beats the smell of real, fresh air.

And then I step onto the bus.

It smells like the inside of an old, dirty sweat

sock. That somebody put a dead rat in. And left in the sun for a month.

And then dragged through a sewer.

It's not too hard to figure out what the cause is, either.

Telly Torkintottintin. The only kid still sitting anywhere near him is Roan Nonaze, and that's only because Roan doesn't have a nose. Lightyear immediately takes off and jumps up on the seat next to Telly. He's in heaven. I guess the stronger the smell the better, as far as Lightyear's concerned.

And then it starts.

"Sme-lly Te-lly! Sme-lly Te-lly!"

It almost seems like he was named Telly for this exact moment. Poor guy. And ol' Larva Boy here knows just how he feels. So I sit down next to Lightyear. I make sure to breathe only through my mouth, a trick I learned when I used to have to use the bathroom right after Grandpa Karl. But that doesn't stop my eyes from watering. And I swear I can actually taste the odour.

"You don't have to sit here. I know how awful it is."

"How awful what is?"

"C'mon, Kelvin. I'm not stupid."

"Eh, it's not *that* bad. But now that you mention it, what's going on? We sit by each other in Professor Plutz's class every day, and I've never noticed anything. Did you fall in something out there, or what?"

"Nah. Nothing like that. It's just that when I feel threatened, my body secretes this liquid as a kind of self-defence. I can't control it. I think it activated when Mr. Jeddee was attacked by that worm."

Wow. Note to self—never pop out from around a corner and surprise Telly. Lightyear sure doesn't seem to mind, though. He loves Telly. Actually, I think he's all right, too. I mean, besides the gag-tacular odour.

"So how come I never see you around after school?"

 "Well, I'm pretty busy taking lessons."

"Really? What kind? Do you play an instrument or something?"

 "Nah."

"Well, what then?"

 "I'd rather not say."

"C'mon, Telly. I promise I won't tell anybody if you don't want me to."

"Yeah, but somebody might hear."

 "There's no one within fifteen feet of us right now. Remember? The whole self-defence odour thing?"

 "Dance."

 "What?"

 "I take dance lessons. Now go ahead and make fun of me."

"Why would I do that? I'm sort of doing the same thing. In fact, Zot's coming over tonight to try to teach me a few moves so I don't look like an idiot at the Galactic Getdown. Well, not as *big* of an idiot, anyway. I'm trying to impress somebody."

"**Wait. Zot is trying to help you impress someone *else*?**"

"**Yeah. We're pretty good friends, you know.**"

"**Sure. I guess. Well, good luck with that. And, Kelvin?**"

"**Yeah?**"

When I got back home after the field trip, I started feeling a little guilty about my sponge idea for Mom's birthday present. Especially since I got her the same thing last year. I couldn't waste the opportunity to grab Luna's attention with the glowing stone, though, so I invited Rand-El over to help me with another idea.

"Cottage cheese? You fed Lightyear cottage cheese?"

"Sure, Rand-El. I figured, what mom
wouldn't be moved to tears by having her son give her a barfed-up ball
of cottage cheese for her birthday?
Jeez. He must have eaten that before
I brought him in here."

"Well, how was I supposed to
know? Besides, maybe your mom
loves barfed-up cottage cheese
balls. You Earth folks can be a little strange, you know."

"Yeah, I don't think so. And I don't
think she'd be too thrilled with any
of these other ones we tried, either."

"Actually, the glass one isn't half
bad."

143

"I guess. But it's not glowing. None of them are glowing like the real one."

I'm getting desperate enough that I'm about to let Lightyear chow down on my original participation trophy, the one he made all the copies from. It's gold with a marble base, so I figure it might make a cool barfed-up stone, even if it is only plastic. But just as I'm about to make the ultimate athletic sacrifice, there's a knock on my bedroom door.

KELVIN, YOU HAVE COMPANY.

"Hey, what are you guys doing here?"

"We're here to teach you how to dance,

remember?" Zot's smile is even wider than usual. And her braces are brighter than any of the duplicate stones Lightyear has been . . . producing. Maybe I should ask Zot to sacrifice her mouthware for the sake of my mom's happiness.

Rand-El looks disgusted. Even more so than usual. "Dance? Why would you want to do something dumb like that? Are you trying to impress somebody, or what?"

"You do know the school dance is in three days, right?" I tell him. "And Principal Ort said he expects to see *everybody* there. What are you going to do, stand in the corner the whole time and pick your nose?"

"Maybe. I just might scratch my butt, too. It would be a heck of a lot more fun than *dancing*. Who wants to do that?"

"Me," Grimnee says as she turns on my music pod and lumbers toward the middle of the room.

"What's going on in there?" It's Dad. "Did you accidentally teleport a herd of pole-vaulting bison into your room, or what? HAR!!"

Zot, Rand-El, and even Grimnee laugh out loud. Nope. I'll never understand.

"Sorry, Dad. We'll try to keep it down."

"Okay," I say to Zot, "how do you want to do this?"

She grabs my hands and leads me to a spot free of Grimnee dance debris.

"There's nothing to it, really. The key is to not be self-conscious and just have fun."

 "Hey, this is great! I hope Luna is as good a dancer as you are, Zot."

AND THAT'S WHY I DON'T LIKE DANCING.

Well, now! This is more like it! Finally someone recognizes the brilliance, the might, the _majesty_ of Erik Failenheimer! Not to mention my leadership capabilities. When these . . . whatever the heck they are . . . saw me roaming around back there, they obviously could sense my aura of magnificence. And what about that rock formation bearing my likeness? Never have I laid eyes upon a more beautiful landscape! Although, I must admit, it _is_ a strange coincidence.

But I wonder—what is the meaning of all this? What do they want from me?

Wait. One of them is approaching my throne.

He looks like he might be their leader. Or might have **been** their leader before I arrived.

"Who are you? And why have you chosen me? Not that I blame you, of course. I'm an excellent choice for . . . whatever it is you chose me for."

" . . . "

"Hello?! Do you understand anything I'm saying? I hope you don't expect me to just sit here and stare at your blank, silent faces all day."

" . . . "

"Zarfloots, man! Don't just stand there like an imbecile! Do _something!_"

There, it looks like that got things going. He's motioning for me to follow him. But where?

We're winding our way back through the village, to a cave at the base of the handsome rock formation.

Now he's taking the torch from its stand and leading me inside. I don't know what he intends to show me, but whatever it is must be pretty important. Guards are posted every twenty feet along the wall.

All right, this is getting ridiculous now.

counting our trek through the village, I've
been walking for _at least_ five minutes
already. And the cave floor is cold. And a
little damp. This is no way to treat an evil
genius who you have just given a crown and
robe to, for Pete's sake! It's time to demand
I be carried the rest of the way and . . .
wait! The torch is illuminating something
there on the wall.

What the . . . _that's me!_ But these etchings
look ancient! Yet, there I am, crash-landing
onto this very planet! And seated on the
throne! And leading this planet's inhabitants

into battle! And . . . could it be? <u>YES!</u> That's me, the master of all I survey, holding the zorb aloft as these curvy creatures grovel at my feet!

This proves it. I am <u>destined</u> to rule the universe! It has been foretold! I will lead my army of minions . . . no, <u>pinions</u> . . . against those who dare to oppose me, and stake my rightful claim to the all-powerful zorb! <u>NOTHING CAN STOP ME NOW!!</u> BWAHAHAHA!!!

OOPS. NOW WHY DID I GO AND SAY *THAT*?

HORRIBLE THINGS HAPPEN WHENEVER I DO.

Well, that was a rough morning. My back still hurts from Zot's dance "lesson" yesterday. So does my hip. And my neck. And both elbows. Even my nostrils are sore. Man, I just don't understand girls.

Everybody but Grimnee is here, so I ask about their ideas for getting rid of the Zorb.

"Your dad's lab is on the bottom level of the space station, right? Well, all we have to do is go outside, cut a hole in the floor, lower the containment vault out of the lab, take it over to a black hole, and dump it in. Problem solved.

Any questions?"

"Um . . . a couple. How do we cut the hole? How do we transport the Zorb? How do we find the nearest black hole? And how do we know that throwing the Zorb into that black hole won't destroy the galaxy?"

"Hey, that's for somebody else to figure out. I'm strictly an idea man."

"Yeah, a *bad* idea man."

"I suppose you can do better?"

"Sure. In my plan we build a time machine, and I get in it, travel back to five minutes before right now, and stuff a sock in your mouth so we don't have to listen to that ridiculous plan."

 "Hey, c'mon, you guys. Cool it. I know we're all a little tense right now, but let's just listen to what everybody has to say. You never know when an idea might lead to a real solution. How about you, Zot? What have you got?"

"Nothing."

 "Really? It's all hands on deck here, Zot. We need everybody's help."

 "Whatever."

Nope. *Definitely* don't understand girls. This isn't going as well as I hoped.

 "How about you, Brian? Are you getting anywhere on the design of that Zorb energy-neutralization beam thingy?"

"It's no use, guys. I've tried everything I can think of to stay calm enough to work on it, but it's no use. All I end up with is a belly full of pickles."

Well, that about does it. Grimnee's not here, and Mippitt isn't programmed for strategic thinking, so that leaves old Spotcho as our last hope for a good idea.

 "Oh, I have a *great* idea. Unfortunately, it has nothing to do with the Zorb. I figured we had enough man-power dedicated to the Zorb issue last night, so I focused on coming up with an idea for your one big thing, Kelvin. Your reputation changer. And I've got it. C'mon, follow me."

Sure. Why not? Since it looks like I'll be mining grismak crystals the rest of my life, I may as well do it with a good reputation.

"So, explain to me again what this thing is."

"It's called an anechoic chamber." I think Spotch is losing his patience with me, but it's hard to tell with his lack of facial expression. "My mom uses it a lot for her acoustics experiments."

"Acoustics?" I sure wish that Mighty Mega Supergeniusness would kick in, so I didn't have to feel so clueless about so many things. I mean, Bula got hers and she's only four. I still haven't figured out how *that's* fair.

"You know, the study of sound. That's my mom's scientific specialty. Her lab down here is filled with cool stuff like this chamber."

"Yeah, I see that. But you said this could be my reputation changer. My one big thing. How's that going to work?"

"Okay, here's the deal." I can tell Spotch is serious now. Not from the tone of his voice, because that hardly ever changes, but because he's grabbed me by the shoulders.

"An anechoic chamber is designed to be absolutely quiet. All those cone shapes covering the walls and ceiling absorb sound waves. You don't get any noise reflecting off the surfaces. No echoes. When you're in there with the door shut, the only sounds you hear are the ones you make yourself. There's no background noise of any kind. It's almost like being out in space."

"Got it." And I really think I do this time. "But I still don't see how this is going to help me."

"Look over there." Spotch points toward a sign on the side of the chamber.

"My mom says the lack of sound will make you freak out after a while. You'll begin to feel strange and maybe even start hallucinating when you've been in there for too long. Forty-two minutes is the longest anyone's been able to last. Kelvin, that can be your name on that sign!"

Now we're talking! Sit on a chair in a nice, quiet room for forty-three minutes and change my reputation forever! This sure beats eating larvae.

"Let's do it!"

I step into the chamber. The only thing inside is a chair. I sit down on it.

"There's a timer on the door. It'll start when I shut it and stop when I open it back up, so we'll have a record of how long you're in there. There's a microphone in the chamber, so if you can't take it anymore, just let me know."

Fat chance. I'm going to put this record so far out of reach, it'll last forever!

I was right! This is going to be a breeze. It really is ridiculously quiet in here, though. So quiet I can hear the buzz of the . . .

. . . lights! What happened to the lights?!

"By the way." It's Spotch. He must have a microphone. "The record is for staying in there in the dark."

"Now you tell me."

My voice sounds weird. It's weaker than usual and seems to just disappear. Must be those cones gobbling up all the sound waves. It makes it feel like I'm in some huge, open space.

The darkness is definitely creepy, but I decide to stick it out and take my shot at glory. Courageous Kelvin has a lot better ring to it than Drifting Doofus. Or Larva Boy. Or Genius.

I close my eyes, which makes things seem a little more normal. But it's *so* quiet in here. I guess you never realize how many little sounds are always going on in the background until they aren't there anymore.

I know, maybe I'll just take a little nap and wake up to a new record. I *am* pretty tired, and it would be so easy to just sort of . . . sort of . . . doze. . . .

BA-DUMP!   BA-DUMP!

BA-DUMP!

Whoa, what's that? It sounds like it's coming from right here next to me, but . . . wait a minute! It's my *heart!* I can feel it now.

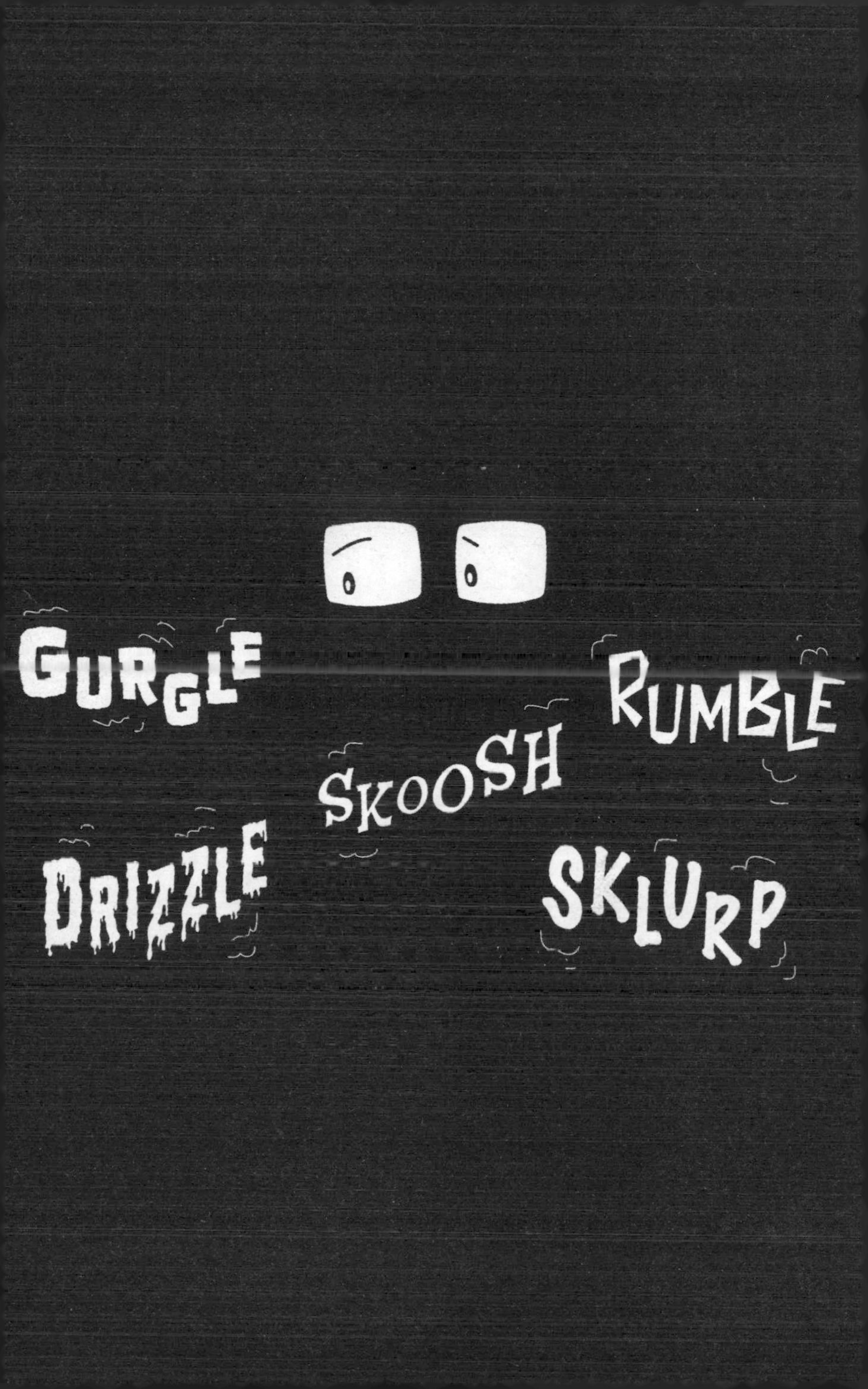
GURGLE
RUMBLE
SKOOSH
DRIZZLE
SKLURP

And that's my *stomach!* Wow. Sounds more like a backed-up sewer drain! My ears must be hunting for things to hear. Spotch was right. The only sounds in here are the ones I make. But who knew I was this loud? And disgusting?

I wiggle my ears and hear a scratching noise. The hair in my ears rubbing on my eardrums? I blink and hear the goopy sound of my eyelids sliding over my eyeballs. When I move my hand, I swear I can hear my wrist bones rubbing together.

SHKRINK!

PLOP!

BBBRRRRAAAPPPP!

SHPURFLISH

GLURP!

SCRAAAAPH!

SNORTCH!

SPLORK!

FRAAAP!

KERPOOSH!

PURFLUTZ!

That's it. I open my eyes and let out a shout . . . that just sort of disappears into the nothingness. Am I even in the chamber anymore? It feels like I'm drifting around in . . . *nowhere*. This is Spotch's fault! He did this! The whole thing was just an excuse to get rid of me. And everybody was in on it. My so-called friends, Principal Ort, the teachers, the lunch ladies, everybody! Even my family, including Bula! *Especially* Bula! What would three geniuses want with an ignoramus who brings the family IQ down?

When I dozed off, they must have shot me into space to spend the rest of my life drifting aimlessly throughout the galaxy! Well, they're all going to be sorry when they realize I'm gone for good. They're going to miss old ignoramus Kelvin. They're going to wish they had let me out when they had the chance. That they had let me out!

"LET ME OUT!"

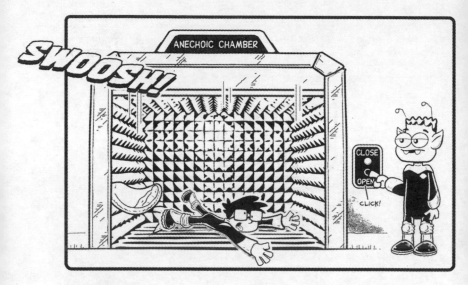

 "Wh-what's going on?"

"You wanted to get out, so I let you out. You seem a little upset. Are you all right?"

 "Uh . . . yeah, sure. No problem. I think I dozed off there for a while, though. Hey, how long was I in there? Did I make it to forty-three?"

"Well . . . sort of."

 "Seconds? **Forty-seven** *seconds?"*

"It looks like Rezbar Gleeyak's
record is safe for a while. Sorry it
didn't work out, Kelvin."

 "Oh, well. At least this time nobody
was around to see me blow it."

"Yeah. About that."

"I figured you'd want everybody to see you do your one big thing, so I sort of broadcast it to the cafeteria. I guess that was a mistake."

 "Bula?! Wh-what are you doing at my school?"

 "Mom brought me for orientation. What's going on?"

 "Nothing. Don't worry about it."

 "It doesn't *look* like nothing. It *looks* like you're embarrassing yourself again. Like the time Mom

caught you kissing that yearbook
picture of Cindy Sloffman."

Oh no! *PLEASE* no! This *cannot* be happening!

"You better not humiliate me like
this when I start going here next
week, Kelvin. After all, I have a
reputation to consider."

And I have a new identity with a new family at

a new school on an ice planet in the next galaxy to consider. If Spotch could show any emotion, I'm sure he'd look sorry right about now. But not as sorry as me.

 "Well, it looks like I'm oh for three in the make-a-new-name-for-myself department."

"I wouldn't say that."

"See?"

"Yup. I'll bet Luna can't wait to hit the dance floor with ol' Larva Boy."

"Oh, c'mon, Kelvin. Once she sees you out there, she'll be begging for you to ask her. You *are* going to use those new moves Zot taught you, right?"

"Only if I wear a helmet. As soon as I told her I needed her help so I could dance with Luna, our lesson sort of . . . took a turn for the worse. I don't get it."

"You don't? Zot likes you, Kelvin."

"I like her, too. So what?"

"No, I mean she *likes* likes you. Haven't you noticed how she's always smiling at you?"

"Zot's *always* smiling. At *everybody*."

Yikes.

Oh, this day just keeps getting better and better. What next? I accidentally swallow my backpack? Or I could get stuck on another elevator with lunch-special guy. Or maybe I slip on a banagal peel, get sucked out an air lock, drift into a wormhole portal, and wind up on the other end of the galaxy on a planet filled with Bula clones. I mean, why not, right?

At least Dorn has stuck to verbal-only bullying ever since Grimnee wrapped him in that wad of desks. It was getting pretty old being crammed into my helmet every day. And rough on my back.

But something seems a little different with Dorn today. I better tread lightly.

 "Uh . . . hey, Dorn. What's up?"

"What's up is I've been named the new captain of the helmet inspec-tion police."

 "What? There's no such thing as the helmet inspection police."

"Wrong again, Genius. Don't worry about it, though. I'm going to help you inspect yours *real* good."

THWUSH!

KLUNK!

THERE. NOW YOU SHOULD BE ABLE TO GET A NICE, CLOSE-UP LOOK.

Aw, c'mon. Are we really back to this again? Dorn must have a death wish.

 "Grimnee's not going to like this!"

"Sorry, Genius, but it's just you and me. Your little bodyguard went to see the doctor."

What'd *I* do? I guess at this end of the galaxy it's a crime to get stuffed into your own space helmet. Well, at least I should be safe here, what with Principal Ort's office right across the hall. And no other helmets in sight. Although the door *is* closed. And I'm sure Dorn would be just as happy to cram me into that recycle slot over there. Man, how much must he hate me to risk getting taken out by Grimnee like that?

I feel the bench shift slightly. I turn in time to see Dorn leaning down toward me. Maybe he doesn't need to cram me into anything. Maybe he's planning a more basic fist-to-body-part type of interaction. I lean away and close my eyes. I may not have a choice whether or not to *feel* what's coming, but I sure don't have to *look* at it.

"You know," Dorn says, in a surprisingly normal-sounding voice, "I used to be a pretty big deal around here before you showed up."

Hey, no stuffing! No pummeling! I decide to risk it and open my eyes.

"Huh?"

"My mom is the head of security on the space station, so we were one of the first families to come out here. I pretty much ran the show at school. Then you guys started coming in from all over the place."

"You guys?" I ask.

"Yeah, you know, the scientist kids."

"Scientist kids? What's wrong with *us*?"

"What's *not* wrong with you?" Dorn's getting a

little agitated now. "You come in here and you're all so smart and everything and the teachers like you and Principal Ort likes you. Even the lunch ladies like you guys. And it all just makes me want to barf."

"And cram me into my helmet."

"Yup."

"Over and over again."

"Yup."

I can't believe I'm actually having a conversation with Dorn. Don't get me wrong. It still feels sort of like a wildebeest-and-crocodile situation. I just know at some point Dorn is going to lunge at me and drag me under the water. But for now we're actually talking.

"But you seem to hate *me* even more than the other kids. I'm not the only one with a parent who's a scientist."

"Yeah, but you're the only one with two. And all I heard for weeks before you even got here was how you were the smartest kid in the whole galaxy. A real supergenius. 'Be nice to Kelvin,' they said. 'Be sure to make Kelvin feel at home,' they said. Makes me want to stick my finger down my throat."

Again with the regurgitating? It's as if the very thought of me makes Dorn sick to his stomach.

"Actually, it's Mighty Mega Supergenius," I blurt out before I can stop myself.

"What?"

"You called me a supergenius, but I'm actually a Mighty Mega Supergenius." Crap! Stop talking, Kelvin! You're just asking for that croc to drag you down.

"Well, at least I was supposed to be. But it's no secret anymore. You know as well as everybody else—I'm just average."

"If that."

"So why are you still picking on me, then?"

"Because I'm the bully. It's what I do. It's what everybody *expects* me to do. And I can't go letting everybody down, now can I?"

Dorn looks horrified.

 "Uh, I don't think that's such a good idea, Principal Ort."

"Nonsense, Mr. Dorn. It's a wonderful idea. A WONDERFUL idea! A SPECTACULAR idea! A SENSATIONAL idea! Ah, here she comes now."

I glance over at Dorn. He looks even more horrified. And now I can hear voices coming from
inside Principal Ort's office. Actually, it sounds
more like just one voice. One loud voice. One very,
very, very loud voice. And then everything is quiet
for a few seconds before the door slides open and
Dorn's mom appears.

"Let's go," she says to Dorn, glowering.

Dorn pulls himself up off the bench and shuffles along behind her as she heads back down the
corridor. It's just me and Backpack now.

"Hey, Backpack. Why do you let Dorn carry you around everywhere and treat you like that?"

"Oh, it's not so bad. Nobody teases me about being little anymore. And he helps me with my math homework."

"He does? But he's failing math."

"Yeah. I think he doesn't want anybody to know he's good at it. Weird, huh? See you later, Kelvin."

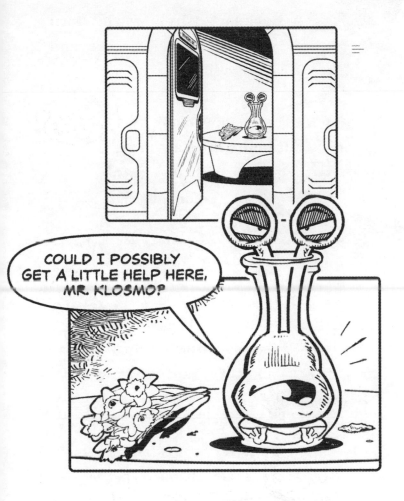

ow, this is the life that I, Erik Failenheimer, was born to live! No longer must
I feel the disappointment, the shame, of coming in second to Klyde and Klara Klosmo. Or
would it be third? Bah! It matters not. Soon
__all__ the universe will bow before my awesome
might. And those cretinous Klosmos will be the
ones fanning my overwhelming gloriousness

with palm fronds. For the remainder of their miserable lives! BWAHAHAHA!!

Imagine their dread as I lead my pinion army against the pathetic defences of the Galactic science Hub! Imagine their horror as I take young Melvin hostage from right under their noses! Imagine their despair as they hand the zorb over to me in ultimate defeat! Imagine my disappointment when I realize I have no way to get my army over to the space station. ZARFLOOTS! What was I thinking?!

I suppose I could take them over one at a time in my Harrowing Handship!!! BWAHA-HAHA!!! (Yup. Still sounds breathtaking.) But that could take weeks, or maybe months. Even Klosmo would suspect something was up. No, I need a vessel large enough to stuff them all into at once. Maybe these pinions are more advanced than they are letting on. Perhaps their ridiculous appearance is not a true indicator of their technological capabilities.

"Brunswick! Front and centre!"

 "Do you possess a ship capable of transporting your entire populace through space?"

 " . . . "

 "Well? Do you?

 " . . . "

196

"speak up, man! I don't have all day!"

"J xjti J dpvme iju zpv xjui b usff csbodi." *(I WISH I COULD HIT YOU WITH A TREE BRANCH.)*

"And there it is. Zarfloots! This language barrier is beginning to chap my hide! Look here, you ignoramus!"

Well, it looks as though my ship isn't the only one to have crash-landed on this planet. And this certainly explains the goofy outfits. These ships don't appear to be too badly damaged, though. With a little TLC, I should have them up and running again in no time. And then . . . <u>NOTHING CAN STOP M</u>—jeez, am I an idiot, or what?

h-oh. There's the bell. I hurry over to my science class and plop down in my usual seat between Spotch and Rand-El. Lucky for me, Mr. Jeddee is late. Even though I'm 99 percent sure of the answer, I ask Spotch if Brian's been able to get anywhere on his beam design since lunch. I figure maybe with a full stomach the thought of it doesn't scare him quite as much. It's actually more hoping than figuring, since nobody else has come up with a different plan.

"See for yourself."

PICKLES!

 "Wow. That might be the smallest I've ever seen his brain."

 "Yup. He was fine, but as soon as I mentioned the Zorb again, he totally stressed out."

The door glides open. It's Mr. Jeddee.

 "My apologies for being late today. I had to shuttle back to the space station in order to pick up a very special visitor."

"Say hello to the professor. He was kind enough to take time out from his busy day in the laboratory to talk to us about a special project he's working on."

"Hello there, everyone. I must say, I was quite, quite, *quite* excited when Mr. Jeddee invited me to your classroom today. I certainly welcome any opportunity to talk about my incredible Growth Ray."

"Cool! So it makes things bigger?"

"No. Smaller."

"Then why did you call it a growth ray?"

"Because that's my name—Professor Growth. But you make a good point. Perhaps to avoid confusion I'll call it my incredible Growth Shrink Ray from now on. Yes, yes, *yes* indeed. I do like the sound of that!"

The professor spends the next twenty minutes explaining all the boring details of his Growth Shrink Ray. At least, it's boring to me, since I don't recognize half the words. Then he answers a few questions from the class ("How long have you been working on it?" "Three hundred twenty-five years." "Why did you invent it?" "Because I wanted to make things smaller"). I'm just about to drift off into another daydream when . . .

 "And now for a little demonstration."

Okay. NOW we're talking! The professor pulls a chair to the front of the classroom and aims the ray at it.

 "At this point the ray only has a range of a few feet. First I set the reduction dial to the desired level of shrinkage. Let's say twenty percent of original size. Then I simply pull this lever and . . ."

"Well, now. That is definitely, definitely, *definitely* not right. Let's take a quick little look-see here. There must be something blocking the randorf cabobbulator."

VZZZZZ!

YUP, YUP, YUP. THAT WAS IT, ALL RIGHT.

Okay. That might have been the best classroom demonstration *ever*! Even better than that time in third grade when Wendy Festnook's mom brought in her supposedly house-trained raccoon troop. It also gave me an idea.

"Hey, Spotch," I whisper. "Are you thinking what I'm thinking?"

"Yeah," he whispers back. "We may not need Brian's brain after all."

You know, this just might work! Every minute that Zorb is on this station, the danger grows. Spotch and I can run our idea by the gang tomorrow and see what's what. But we have to act fast. And we're going to have to take care of everything ourselves.

It's still frustrating knowing that I can't count on Mom and Dad to take this whole thing . . .

. . . seriously.

"Uh . . . what's going on in here?"

"We're getting our boogie on! What's it look like?"

 "It *looks* like you've been watching your *Saturday Night Fever* video-tape again."

"Well then, in this case, looks are not deceiving! Your mom and I left the lab early today to come home and watch it. There's still some synthetic popcorn in the kitchen if you're hungry."

I'm hungry, all right. But not for popcorn-shaped pencil erasers, thank you very much.

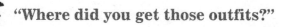 "Where did you get those outfits?"

"Professor Haaarvaaartan let us

borrow the clothing synthesizer
he's been working on. Doesn't
your father look handsome? Just
like John Travolta!"

I recognize John Travolta's name from the movie
poster Dad has hanging in the den back home on
Earth. Mom and Dad have seen that movie at least
fifty times, and they've never done this afterward.
Something must be up.

"Sweetie, come join us. We hear
you're trying to learn how to
dance."

"Bula. Why, is it a secret?"

The little mole must have been listening through the air vents or something yesterday when Zot and Grimnee were over. Funny how even a genius can be an annoying pest when she's your little sister. Even so, I'm definitely not interested in learning dance moves from the Jurassic period. Especially from my mom and dad.

 "Thanks for the offer, but I'm good. So I guess you can take those outfits off and throw them in the trash compactor. And then burn them. And dump the ashes into space."

"What? Then we won't have anything to wear when we chaperone your dance Thoosday."

"Yuppers. We're going to glide and groove like greased geese at the Galactic Getdown! HAR!"

No!
No, no, no, no, no, no, no, no!
No!

"But the dance is right after school. You guys will still be working."

 "Oh, don't you worry. We'll be there. And when we let loose of our sweet moves in front of your classmates, they'll never look at you the same way again!"

Yeah, that's what I'm afraid of.

DAY 6

30

ms. Gassias better not be counting on much class participation this morning. I can hardly keep my eyes open. It's tough to get a good night's sleep when every time your lids close, visions of your parents dancing in front of the whole school fill your head. If you can call what they were doing "dancing." I can't believe anyone actually *did* that. And *dressed* like that when they did it. With my luck, Bula inherited their brains, and I'll get stuck with their dance moves and sense of style.

I'm sitting in the back of the class, with Spotch,

Rand-El, and Brian. Zot's in this class, too, but she's strictly a front-rower, so that the teacher can clearly see her hand raised to answer every question. Grimnee sits up there, too, but her hand stays down on her desk.

We need to talk about our plan to destroy the Zorb, but it looks like that will have to wait until lunch. Somebody just walked into the room, but it's not Ms. Gassias.

GOOD MORNING, CLASS. MS. GASSIAS WON'T BE HERE FOR THE NEXT FEW DAYS, SO I WILL BE SUBSTITUTING FOR HER. MY NAME IS MRS. PPHHFFTT.

MRS. PPHHFFTT

Giggles fill the classroom. I mean, how could they not, right?

"Yes, go ahead and laugh. But I'll have you know that Pphhfftt is the third most popular surname on my planet, right behind Bbrraapp . . ."

Louder giggles.

" . . . and Bblleecchh."

Riotous laughter. One kid even falls out of his chair, but he was pretty slippery to begin with.

"It pleases me that our names bring you all such joy. Hopefully, this writing assignment will as well—a two-page paper titled 'What Gives Me Strength.' I know you have a big dance tomorrow, so we'll make this due the following day."

"A paper? But this is math class."

 "Alas, I am not a *math* teacher. I am a *writing* teacher. And what you will *write* is a paper on what gives you strength."

"You mean like push-ups and stuff? Or protein shakes?"

 "No, I mean your *inner* strength. You all came here from distant worlds to start new lives. What is it that helps you handle everything that is being thrown at you every day? This certainly isn't an easy situation to be in. I'm looking for thoughtful, well-written papers that you can share with the class."

Share with the class? Thoughtful and well

written? Dang. This is definitely *not* going to help me lose my nongenius genius label.

 "As for today, I haven't had time to prepare a lesson, so we'll be watching an informative film."

Mrs. Pphhfftt turns out the lights and starts the informative film. It's called *Hygiene Hints for Space-Bound Students*.

Spotch, Brian, Rand-El, and I all rank pretty high on the cleanliness scale, at least compared to *some* of the kids at this school. So we decide to put the next thirty minutes to better use. We huddle up and go over the revised Zorb Destruction Plan, which is basically the same as Brian's original plan except for one detail.

"Whatever! Tell you what. Let's just call it the Ray That Shrinks Things. How's that?"

 "Actually, that sounds a little awkward."

"Yeah. How about just Shrink Ray? It's a lot simpler and to the point."

"I think what Kelvin's trying to say is we can use the ray to shrink the whole containment vault, with the Zorb inside it, down to nothing."

 "Exactly. But the ray only works at extremely close range, so we have to get in tight. We can use Brian's original idea of having Lightyear hork up a copy of my dad in order to get past the sentry robots. Then we shrink the Zorb until it's gone. Or at least so small that nobody will ever find it. Easy as pie."

"I don't know. I still think we should leave it up to the adults."

 "Already tried that, Rand-El. Now it's on us to do something. And the sooner the better. When we get home today, Spotch and I will get Lightyear to make a copy of my dad. Rand-El, you and Brian get ahold of the Shrink Ray."

"How the heck are we supposed to do that?"

"You'll think of something. Then we'll meet outside my dad's lab at eight o'clock. I still have the duplicate key card from a couple months ago. We can hide the ray and dupli-Dad in the lab until we're ready to use them."

Just then, from somewhere in the room, comes the sound of someone . . . uh . . . cutting the cheese. Very loudly.

31

Ah, it's great to be me! Only I, Erik Failen-heimer, would have the good fortune of the two cargo ships being in near-perfect working order. Just a little fine-tuning and they'll be ready to serve my purposes—capturing Kelvar Klosmo (or whatever his name is), trading him for the Zorb, and taking over the Galactic Science Hub to use as my own orbiting space lair. BWAHAHAHA!!!

But before I launch my awe-inspiring attack, I must appraise the readiness of my

newfound army for battle. I've been working
with my number two, that dolt Brunswick,
on his English. But after nearly three whole
hours of my incomparable instruction, minus
a couple of forty-five-minute nap breaks, he
still hasn't mastered the language. He does
know a few words, though, so it's time to
put my subjects through the paces.

> BRUNSWICK!
> BATTLE FORMATION!

<u>Zarfloots!</u> What these pea-brained pin-
ions lack in intelligence, they more than
make up for with sheer, blinding speed! Those

galactic Goody Two-shoes on the science Hub won't know what hit them! I can actually **smell** the sweet scent of victory in the air! Although that may just be leftover traces of Bula's lip balm on my nose.

BRUNSWICK!
FORWARD MARCH!

Hmm. We'll have to work on that.

"Is this really the best you could do?"

 "He needs to eat enough to convert it into a full-size copy of my dad. Running the food synthesizer over and over was the only thing I could think of."

"Yeah, but did you have to make cheese with it? Couldn't you have picked something more sturdy, like breadsticks or shnorb sprouts?"

"Could have used those suggestions about an hour ago, Spotcho. I guess we'll just have to be extra careful."

It looks like we're as ready as we're going to be, so Spotch gets into position behind Lightyear.

"Remember, you have to make sure he's looking at my dad when he starts eating," I remind him.

"Got it," Spotch replies, and places his hands on either side of Lightyear's head.

"Hey, Dad!" I yell so he can hear me through the closed door. "Can you come in here for a minute?"

And now I hear music playing. It's a little muffled, but I'm pretty sure it sounds like . . .

"Oh, I see you're in your disco outfit again."

"Yes sir!" Dad's forehead is dripping with sweat. "Thought I'd get a little more practice in before I hit the floor for real tomorrow. I wouldn't want to embarrass you out there."

I know he wouldn't *want* to, but I really don't see any way around it. But that's tomorrow's problem. Right now I've got to keep him occupied long enough for Lightyear to scarf down that food pile.

"Actually, Dad, I changed my mind and was wondering if maybe you could teach me a move I could use tomorrow?" Did I really just say that?

"Sure! I knew once you saw a little more of

what I can do, you wouldn't be able to resist. Let's see now, how about we bust a sweet John Travolta move?"

Wow. He's really going to town. I want to laugh. Or maybe cry. Or gouge my eyes out with a fork. But Lightyear isn't done eating yet, so I do my best to act impressed. Like Mom and Dad do when Bula brings home her latest work of art from preschool. We need Dad to stay in the room for a while yet.

During one of his more flamboyant finger points, Dad spots Lightyear. "Whoa. Is that cheese that he's wolfing down? Whatever he comes up with, you better get rid of it pronto, Tonto. We don't want the smell of ralphed-up cheese covering up the glorious scent of my sweaty disco boots, now do we? HAR!"

Uh-oh!

"Okay, Dad. I think I've got it."

"Already? Well, aren't you the fast learner. A chip off the old boogying block! Maybe we should try a few more—"

"No, really, I'm good." I grab Dad's disco finger and lead him toward the door. "I'll practice some more by myself. Thanks for the help!"

No sooner do I manage to get him out the door than Lightyear starts to work his magic.

Sometimes I wish his magic was guessing which card I pulled out of the deck. This is gross.

"Yuck. Are you sure he can do this?"

"Seriously? He made a Grimnee copy out of rock when we were back on that planetoid two months ago. This should be a breeze."

Another few seconds and he's finished. Spotch and I stand Cheese Dad up to get a good look.

 "I have to admit, that's a pretty amazing likeness. I bet he's not as funny as your real dad, though."

"And I bet he's funnier. C'mon, let's cover him up and get him down to the lab. It's almost eight o'clock, and Rand-El and Brian should be meeting us there with the Shrink Ray in a few minutes."

"Watcha got there, son?"

"It's just the cheese that Lightyear spit out. We're going to toss it into the trash compactor on level three."

"Good thinking. And I'll tell you what—I don't want to see what's under that sheet, but I'll bet it isn't pretty."

You said it, not me.

"Ugh. Those security bots don't have odour sensors, do they? That definitely doesn't smell like your dad."

"You haven't been around him after an hour of 'boogying down' in the living room. But no, the sensors are

visual only. And Zot's here to make
sure we've got that covered."

"Whatever."

"She's going to use her mom's make-
up kit to get Cheese Dad's face to
look a little less . . . cheesy."

"Whatever."

Zot digs into her case and gets to work on the
Dad duplicate. She's got lipstick and eyebrow pen-
cils and hair dye and lots of other junk in there.
Boy, I'm glad I'm not a girl.

"By the way, Rand-El, where the
heck is the Shrink Ray?"

"You mean the Growth Ray."

I'm thinking maybe I could be the kid who

shoves Rand-El out of an air lock into space. *That* could be my one big thing.

"Relax, Kelvin. It should be here in a few minutes."

Brian seems pretty confident. If he wasn't, his brain would be the size of a grape right now.

 "Here you go, go, go. One Growth Shrink Ray, at your service. Just make sure I get it back by next weekend. We're going to a shindig, and my wife needs to use it to fit, fit, fit into her party dress. Oh, hey there, Professor Klosmo. How's it going?"

ALL RIGHTY, THEN. I GUESS I'LL SEE YOU LATER.

 "How the heck did you guys manage that?"

"We just asked if your dad could borrow it. Growth wasn't too keen on the idea, so Brian started to stress out, went all small-brain on me, and started talking about how much he likes pickles again. And, wouldn't you know it, ever since Growth shrank his head, he likes pickles, too. Brian offered him one and *voilà!* We've got a Growth Ray ... er ... Shrink Ray."

"Hey, look. There's a note attached to it."

Dear Professor Klosmo,
Or may I call you Klyde? Be sure, sure, sure to charge the ray for at least twelve hours before use. I don't know what your plans for it are, but good luck, Klyde!

Professor Growth

P.S. I assumed you said it was okay to call you Klyde, even though I'm not here to hear it.

"I don't know about you guys, but I can't hang around here for twelve hours! My curfew is nine o'clock!"

 "I guess we'll just have to come back tomorrow night, after the dance. Let's hide everything inside the lab until then."

I pull out the copy of my dad's key card that Lightyear made from Rand-El's retainer two months ago and slide it into the door lock. The door slides open and we can see the Zorb containment vault and the security bots on the far side of the lab. We hide Cheese Dad and the Shrink Ray behind a supply cabinet near the door, connect the ray's cord to a nearby power source, and head back out into the corridor.

I look over at Zot before she leaves. "Thanks a lot for your help, Zot."

"Whatever."

We all head back to our LIV spaces. We have a

big day tomorrow, what with the dance and sav-
ing the universe again and everything. And when I
get back to my room and hop into my zero-gravity
pod for the night, there's one thought that I can't
get out of my head—*Cheese Dad and Shrink Ray*
would be a great name for a buddy cartoon.

DAY 7

OKAY, SO REMEMBER—WE MEET RIGHT BACK HERE AS SOON AS THE DANCE IS OVER. THEN WE'LL HEAD FOR THE BUS, AND MIPPITT WILL SHUTTLE US OVER TO THE SPACE STATION TO SHRINK THE ZORB.

 "Hey, where *is* Mippitt, anyway?"

 "Oh, he's not programmed to dance, so he's waiting for us in the bus. He downloaded the operating manual into his system last night, so he should be good to go."

"I still don't see why we have to wait until after the dance. Why don't we just sneak over there now and skip the stupid thing altogether?"

"Because, Rand-El, my parents are chaperones. Don't you think they'd notice if I wasn't there?"

And I wouldn't get the chance to dance with Luna, but I keep that reason to myself.

"But I signed them up for the cleanup committee, too. So if we wait until after the dance, they'll be stuck here for a while, and we'll have the lab to ourselves."

 "Uh . . . in a little bit. We just got here."

"We can dig it! We'll catch you groovy kids on the flip side. I've gotta *chap* and your mom's gotta *rone*. Klosmos out!"

What . . . was . . . *that*? My reputation is already taking on massive amounts of water, and now they go ahead and fire a massive nuclear homing torpedo of death at it? My only hope is that every-body is into their own thing, so nobody notices them.

What?! Please, please, *please* tell me that most of the kids don't know who they are.

I need to find a new school in another galaxy.

Although, I didn't anticipate how slow we'd be moving. I must have chosen two elderly pinions to pilot the transports. The one behind me has had his left-turn blinker on the entire trip!

I hope to catch Melvin, or whatever his name is, at school, before he returns home to the science Hub. That way I'll only have to deal with a few teachers rather than a space station loaded with security. And robots. And weird rays. Then, once I exchange the boy for the zorb, taking the space station will be a cake walk. Or is it a walk in the park? Or a cake in the park? Ah, who cares.

There's the school now! A little enhancement of my video screen, and we shall see what's what.

Excellent! The little troglodytes should still be here. This is a sure sign that my

luck is finally changing. Now to locate this
getdown.

And there they are!

Giggle-Giggle

Giggle-Giggle-Giggle-Giggle!

There she is. Luna. Should I go talk to her? Of course I should. That is my plan, after all. All right, here I go. No. Wait. What am I thinking? I can't just go over and talk to her. What am I, insane? No, an insane person wouldn't be able to think this clearly. Or maybe an insane person would *think* they're thinking clearly when they're really not. Maybe I should just keep standing by the punch bowl and hope *she* comes over *here*. No, don't be stupid. Why would she come over here? Why? To get some punch, probably. Or to see me. I mean, she *did* ask me if I was coming to the dance, right? Wait, where am I? What time is it? Why are my ears sweating? Am I wearing pants?

"You all right, Kelv? You don't look so good."

"What? Yeah. Huh?"

"Man, you better sit down. I'll grab you some punch."

All right, Kelvin. Calm down. I take a couple deep breaths and my mind starts to clear up. I grab Rand-El by the elbow. Safety in numbers and all.

"I'm okay. C'mon, Rand-El. Let's go see if Luna and her friends want to dance."

"Dance? I'd rather dunk my head
in the punch bowl."

"Well, just come along with me, then.
I can't go over there by myself."

Rand-El lets out a ridiculously overblown sigh,
drops his head, and shuffles along as I drag him
toward the girls. "You owe me," he says.

All right, Kelvin. Pull it together. Think of
something cool to say. You don't want to make a
fool of yourself.

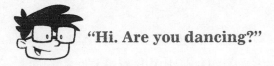 "Hi. Are you dancing?"

Ugh.

 "Excuse me, what?"

 "No, of course you're not. I meant, uh, would you *like* to dance?"

 "Not really. I think dancing's kind of stupid."

 "I know, right?!"

 "I mean, look at this hair. Would *you* want to jump around and get it all sweaty and messy?"

 "Of course not!"

Well, I wasn't expecting this. I don't really have

a backup plan for this situation. I barely had a regular plan. I decide to go straight to the big guns.

 "I found this on our field trip. What do you think?"

"I think it's a rock."

 "Well . . . you can have it if you want."

"Gee, really? I can have a rock? From Larva Boy? How lucky am I?"

"Not very, if you ask me."

 "Hey, you're pretty funny. And kinda cute, too."

Oh, man. I've got to get out of here.

 "C'mon, Rand-El. Let's go."

"You go on, Kelvin. I'm going to hang out here for a while."

Seriously? I put the stone back in my pack and walk away. King Kong on the Empire State Building wasn't shot down as hard as I just was.

I see Zot standing by herself near the punch bowl, so I head on over to a friendly face. Well, what used to be a friendly face.

"Hey, Zot."

"Kelvin? What are you doing here? Shouldn't you be out there dancing with Luna?"

"It turns out she doesn't like to dance. It also turns out she doesn't like me."

"You don't say."

"I do say. I don't get it, either. I mean, she specifically asked me if I was coming to the dance."

"She specifically asked *everybody*. She's in charge of refreshments and needed to know how many cookies to order."

"Well, how was I supposed to know that? Now I really feel like an idiot. I mean, she was hardly even paying attention when I was talking to her."

"I could have told you that, Kelvin. Luna is all about Luna."

"I don't know about that." I glance over toward Luna's gang.

"She seems to be having a pretty good time with Rand-El," I say.

"Yeah," says Zot. "Probably because he has six eyes to stare at her with."

We both chuckle at that one. Zot seems to be breaking out of her mood a bit.

"So, how come you're not out there dancing?" I ask her.

"Nobody I want to dance with has asked me yet."

"Wait a minute. You're just standing around waiting for the right guy to ask you to dance? The Zot Totzie I know would just grab him and haul him out there."

"You know what? You're right!"

"Let's see some of those moves I taught you."

"Like that flip onto my head?"

"Yeah. Sorry about that."

"That's all right. I deserved it. Look, Zot. I'm really sorry. I had no idea you—"

"Kelvin?"

"Yeah?"

"Shut up and dance."

I'm with Zot, Grimnee, and Brian at the refreshment table. I guess Luna can't count, because they're out of cookies already. And the punch is almost gone, too, because Zot is guzzling it. I guess you work up quite a thirst dancing like she does.

"Hey," she tells me between gulps, "you weren't bad out there. I guess I'm a pretty good teacher."

"Yeah, you and Telly Torkintottintin."

"Who?" Zot looks confused.

"The kid I got to know on the field trip. He

showed me a few things, too. And none of his were head-cracking moves."

Uh-oh. Speaking of head cracking . . .

 "Relax. I'm not here to cause any trouble."

"Really? What else do you know how to do?"

 "Well, I . . . um . . . I guess I was sort of wondering if . . . you know . . . maybe Grimnee wouldn't mind dancing with me too much."

Well, what do you know. This has been a pretty crazy afternoon, but I can't imagine anything topping that.

What the . . . ?! That's Bula's plushy, Fluffles!
And he's . . . *talking*?!

"That's him! That's the same voice I heard back when we were trapped in that giant robot! That's the guy who was trying to take the Zorb off that planetoid!"

Okay. Dorn asking Grimnee to dance seems pretty normal now.

"But we sent him drifting aimlessly through space. How did he end up back here?"

AH. HERE WE GO.

"Behold the awesome might of Erik Failenheimer!"

"Failenheimer? I'm pretty sure that was the name of the janitor who was on the shuttle from Earth with us. What the heck is going on?"

"Listen very carefully, do exactly as I say, and no one will be hurt. At least not until I gain the universe-shattering power I so richly deserve. Then all bets are off!"

 "Universe-shattering power? Kelvin, he must be after the Zorb again!"

"When I arrive in fifteen minutes, you will hand Melvin Klosmo over to me immediately. Until then, feel free to sit there and contemplate living out the remainder of your days under the iron-fisted rule of the almighty Erik Failenheimer! BWAHAHAHA!!!"

"Melvin Klosmo? He must mean me. He must be planning on using me to get the Zorb somehow. Quick, Brian, gather everybody together!"

THIS PUNCH NEEDS MORE PICKLES!

 "Okay. Scratch Brian. Quick, Zot, gather everybody together. We've got fifteen minutes to get over to the space station and shrink that Zorb!"

Only fifteen minutes. Mippitt better be able to fly that shuttle like a rocket. The gang's all together, so we bolt for the door.

"All right, Spotch. It's me he wants, so I'll try to stall him. You sneak out of here with Rand-El and Brian and get to the bus. You guys have to shrink the Zorb before it's too late."

They make their way to the door on the other side of the gymnasium. Bula's bunny doesn't seem to care. He's focused on me. And it's pretty creepy. But I need to distract him as long as I can to give Spotch and the guys a chance to do their stuff.

"I thought you said you'd be here in fifteen minutes."

There. That's a good start.

 "I lied. I'm a bad guy. It's what we do."

Well, that's all I've got. I hope those seven seconds gave Spotch and the guys the time they needed.

"I AM NOT A JANITOR! I am a brilliant scientist who has been forced unjustly to live in your horrible, joke-telling shadow for my entire professional career!"

"Well, I remember them giving you a bucket and mop when we first got here. What's your area of scientific expertise, anyway? Toilet cleanliness? HAR!"

Now *that's* how you stall.

"Laugh while you can, you insufferable simpleton, but my moment is at hand. Zarfloots, Brunswick! I didn't bring you along for your witty repartee! Grab the Klosmos!"

"what in the name of frozen molasses is going on here, Brunswick?! why are they plodding around like newborn elephants? where are their catlike reflexes? where is their _cheetah–like speed?_"

"..."

"I forgot for a moment that I'm trying to communicate with a fence post. Let's try this again. WHY. SO. SLOW?"

"Hard to move. Feel heavy."

"Feel heavy?! What, did you swallow a bag of anvils on the way over here? No, I think the problem is that you're just a bunch of lazy—wait a minute! It's the gravity! The artificial gravity on this floating space school is much stronger than you're used to back on your planet. I can't believe I didn't think of that!"

"What, no 'HAR'?"

"It wasn't a joke."

"You know what else isn't a joke? Part two of my diabolical plan! Brunswick, bring them to me. No, wait! Something isn't right. What do you have in that pack?"

THIS? JUST SOME STUFF.

 "JUST some <u>stuff</u> you plan on using to try and defeat me, no doubt! BRUNSWICK, see what's in that pack!"

"Where do you think you're going?! Get back here!"

Dad and I look at each other, stunned.

"What the heck is that thing, Kelvin?"

"I don't know. I found it on the field-trip planet. I thought it was just a cool rock."

"Well, those goofy, pin-shaped fellas are scared to death of it. Almost like they're natural enemies."

The boball begins to make a strange sound and starts rocking back and forth. It looks like it's about to . . .

 "Why are you always bunching together? Spread out! How many times did we go over this?!"

"Well, son, it looks like we won't have to worry about those nitwits anymore. As a matter of fact, I'm not sure we ever did. Leave it to Erik Failenheimer to put together an army of simpleminded, easily toppled scaredy-cats."

 "Don't forget slow-moving."

I ALREADY TOLD YOU—THEY WEREN'T SLOW-MOVING UNTIL THEY GOT HERE!

FLING!

"They were merely a distraction anyway. The real prize is waiting for us over in your laboratory, isn't it, Klosmo? Get moving if you ever want to see young Klevlin again."

"It's Kelvin."

"Whatever."

At the Klosmo Laboratory . . .

DINK! DINK!

"Remember, one false move and I turn Mervin here into a stink-bug."

"You invented a ray that turns people into stinkbugs? No wonder they made you a janitor."

"Go on. Keep it up. I'll be giving you a position far worse than janitor once I rule the universe."

"Yeah, about that. Do you have any idea how big the universe really is?"

"Of course I do! I'm a brilliant scientist . . ."

"Janitor."

". . . and once I have the zorb, nothing will be out of my reach!"

"Don't worry, Dad. He won't get the Zorb. We made sure of that."

"What are you babbling about?"

"You'll see, as soon as we turn this . . ."

LITTLE HELP?

 ". . . corner."

"Security bots—scan me for iden-tification and then return to se-cure monitoring status."

"The Zorb's still here! What happened to the Shrink Ray plan??!"

"Brian got hungry and ate a chunk of the Cheese Dad's face. The bots didn't recognize him, so they trapped us."

"I ran out of pickles."

 "All right. Everybody step away from the zorb. klosmo, deactivate the security bots."

"Nope. You can do whatever you want to me, but I'll never let you take it."

"oh, but it isn't you who'll be spending the rest of his life as a stinkbug. You'll be spending the rest of your life as the _father_ of a stinkbug! unless, of course, you aren't careful where you step. BWAHAHAHA!!!"

"It's okay, Dad. I'm just a Drifting Doofus, Under-a-Minute Moron, Larva Boy nongenius genius anyway. What's adding stinkbug to the list going to do? Who knows, maybe I'll even end up being popular in the stinkbug community."

"If you turn Kelvin into a stinkbug, you'll have to turn all of us into stinkbugs!"

"Yeah! Do stinkbugs like pickles?"

"Are you kidding me? A stinkbug?! Have you guys taken the
time to think this through? I
mean, they're called STINKbugs
for a reason! Okay. I'm in."

"Nobody is going to be turned into
a stinkbug. Security bots—scan
me for identification and then
deactivate for five minutes. Go
ahead and take the Zorb, Failenheimer. I'm betting a ten-inch-
tall, cotton-filled janitor won't be
able to use it anyway."

"What's the matter, Klosmo? No
'HAR'? I happen to think this whole
situation is hilarious."

"Just take the containment vault

and go. If you try to open it here, I'll reactivate the security bots. We're not about to be turned into goo."

42

HOW COULD YOU DO THAT? YOU JUST GAVE THE MOST POWERFUL OBJECT IN THE UNIVERSE TO AN INSANE PLUSHY!

"Ah, don't worry about it. That wasn't the real Zorb. It was just a big papier-mâché balloon that Bula painted in her art class. The real Zorb is over there, in the corner. In the real containment vault."

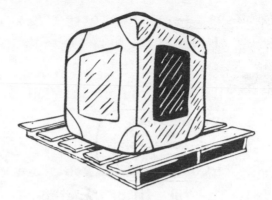

 "The *real* Zorb? The *real* containment vault? But that means the security bots were guarding the fake Zorb instead of the real one!"

 "Yup. It's called hiding in plain sight. And it's the oldest trick in the book. By the time our cushy little custodian figures out what happened, it'll be too late."

 "Too late? Dad, he's just going to come back and try to steal it again."

"Well, he can try, but there won't be anything here to steal."

 "What do you mean? The Zorb is right over there."

"Not for long. Kelvin, you were right. The Zorb *is* too dangerous! I see that now. And I'm sorry for not taking you seriously before. I really did think we could study it and harness its power and accomplish great things. And maybe we could have. But if a ten-inch-tall stuffed nitwit like Failenheimer could cause this much trouble, I don't even want to think about what an actual, competent evil genius would do."

"So what are you going to do with it, Professor?"

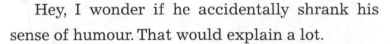

"Me? Nothing. You guys are the ones with the plan. Go ahead and use it. Besides, I wouldn't want to accidentally shrink my suit. It's a little too tight in the backside already. HAR!"

Hey, I wonder if he accidentally shrank his sense of humour. That would explain a lot.

Spotch, Rand-El, and I wheel the Shrink Ray over to the real containment vault. Brian is following behind with the partially eaten Cheese Dad on the hand truck. He's chewing on something that looks like an elbow.

"I bet he'd be great at catching mice! HAR!"

Rand-El aims the ray. Spotch sets the dial to 0 percent of original size. Brian sniffs Cheese Dad. And I pull the lever.

43

I don't know how they managed to escape the school and get back here without me, but their efforts were all for naught. Little do Brunswick and the rest of those pea-brained pinions know, but their celebration

is about to end. Once I open the containment vault, nothing that lives can survive
being this close to the all-powerful Zorb
without transforming into a puddle of goo.
And in their case, I must say it would be
an improvement. Fortunately for me, my tiny
little plushy body won't be affected!

The dolts have served their purpose, though,
so now it's time to make those cave draw-
ings come true! It's time for me to wield the
Zorb and become the most powerful being in
the universe! NOTHING CAN STOP ME NOW!!

307

Epilogue

 "So what was the deal with that weird little guy with the big ears yesterday? He and that group of wobbly goofballs with him were the highlight of the dance!"

"I know, right? They said the whole thing was an act. Part of the entertainment."

The "they" they're talking about would be my dad. He thinks the other kids would be better off not knowing about things like the Zorb. He thinks they have enough to deal with out here in space without worrying about things like being turned into goo or being enslaved by a power-hungry plushy. Maybe he's right, but I don't think he's giving us kids enough credit.

Either way, the rest of the gang and I are sworn to secrecy. Which means no one will know I helped save the universe. Again. It also means that instead of being an intergalactic hero, I'll continue to be Larva Boy. Or the Drifting Doofus. Or Genius. Maybe I'll write a book about all this someday. Although, with my luck, they'll probably put it in the fiction section.

Of course it doesn't.

 "Mr. Klosmo, we'll begin with you."

Of course we will.

I hate writing theme papers. I spent an hour last night just staring at my blank tablet screen. Zilcharino. Then I overheard Mom reading Bula her favourite bedtime book, and it gave me an idea. So I decided to go a different route. I figured I might as well go for it. It's not like a kid they call

Larva Boy has much to lose anyway. Right? I guess
we'll see.

My reputation when I got here
Was that I was really smart.
But instead of being honest,
I thought I could *act* the part.

Well, that was a disaster,
As I'm sure you're all aware,
Because I'm barely average
When it comes to mental flare.

So now I'm teased by everyone.
Well, almost, I should say,
Because there are some classmates
Who've stuck with me all the way.

First, there's Gil Lagoonie,
Who's a friendly, happy soul.
How hard it all must be for him
To live inside that bowl.

And Brian's brain is on display
inside a plastic globe.
We all know when he's nervous,
'Cause it shrinks his frontal lobe.

Zot is full of energy,
Enough to light a moon.
She's so graceful and athletic
That I feel like a buffoon.

Rand-El is the only kid
With glasses on his planet.

Some kids call him Twelve Eyes.
That can't be too pleasant, can it?

Spotch is pretty even keeled,
He's rarely up or down.
It's really hard to make him smile,
Harder yet to make him frown.

Grimnee doesn't say too much,
A chatterbox she's not.
But if you are a bully,
She will squash you on the spot.

Mippitt's brain is made of circuits.
He's got wires instead of veins.
He mainly beeps and whistles,
But I like him just the same.

And Dorn was quite the bully.
He would terrorize the school,
But Grimnee put an end to that
And now Dorn's pretty cool.

So the answer's right in front of me,

I had it all along,

Because having awesome friends

Is the thing that makes me strong.

Oh, man. That sounded *way* less lame in my head before I actually read it out loud. Kelvin, you're such a putz! D minus, here I come. And if I thought the teasing was bad before, I'm going to have to wear my helmet to class to deflect the bombs coming my way after this disaster.

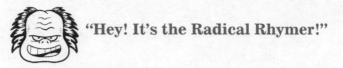 **"Hey! It's the Radical Rhymer!"**

The Radical Rhymer? Yeah, I guess I can live with that. At least until my Mighty Mega Super-geniusness kicks in.

The Pinion Language

Now that you've finished the book, you probably noticed that the pinions didn't always have their comments translated into English. Wouldn't you just love to know what they were saying? Well, you can! Just replace each pinion language letter with the one that comes right before it in the alphabet. So, for example, replace a pinion *d* with *c*, a pinion *s* with *r*, and so on. If you encounter a pinion *a*, replace it with a *z*. Fbtz qfbtz!

Acknowledgements

We would like to thank the wonderful JIMMY crew for all their help in publishing this book. It takes a lot of hard work from a lot of dedicated and talented people to bring a hybrid project like this into the world, and these folks do a fantastic job. To our editor, Aubrey Poole, as well as to Tracy Shaw, Stephanie Yang, Sabrina Benun, Gabrielle Tyson, Ben Allen, Erica Stahler, Michelle Gengaro, and all those who work behind the scenes: our sincere thanks and major kudos to you all.

And, as always, continued thanks to our super agent, Dan Lazar, and everyone at Writers House, especially Cecilia de la Campa and Victoria Doherty-Munro. You guys are the best.

About the Authors

John Martin is the illustrator of the Vordak the Incomprehensible series. A day doesn't go by without him drawing monsters, robots, and characters from his childhood. He lives in Michigan with his wife, Mary; sons, Adam and Paul; and daughter, Grace.

Scott Seegert is the author of the Vordak the Incomprehensible series. If you didn't know better, and couldn't see him, you would swear he was twelve years old. He lives in Michigan with his wife, Margie; sons, Brad and Jason; and daughter, Shannon.